PREACHER
OF THE PECOS

PREACHER OF THE PECOS

C. E. EDMONSON

aventine press

Published by Aventine Press
55 East Emerson St.
Chula Vista, CA 91911

ISBN: 978-1-59330-955-8

Library of Congress Control Number: 2019938137
Library of Congress Cataloging-in-Publication Data
Preacher Of The Pecos

www.ceedmonson.com

Love bears all things, believes all things, hopes all things, endures all things.
—1 Corinthians 13:7

CHAPTER 1

Cole Bradhurst crossed the Pecos River at the Norton ford, one of the few places along the river's nine hundred miles where the currents and steep muddy banks allowed an easy passage. The Pecos was shallow here, shallow enough for wagons to roll across, and solid underfoot, a welcome relief from the sandy bottom found along most of its length.

On the far side, Elijah Norton's farm stretched north, south, and west, with hundreds of acres under cultivation, most given over to alfalfa, corn, and other local produce. Behind Cole, on the eastern side of the river, browned grass, cactus, and scrub extended across the flat tableland to the horizon.

Once safe on the western bank, Cole dismounted and led his horse toward a small corral where Elijah was bent over a new fence post he hoped to have in place before dusk. Cole wore a simple gray shirt with a bib front, a leather vest, and denim pants of the type made famous by Mr. Levi in California. His boots were well worn, as was the black hat pulled low over his eyes. While a rifle, a Winchester by the look of it, rested in a scabbard attached to the saddle of his horse, he was not wearing a handgun.

"How do," Cole called out as he approached the corral. Tucked behind a barn, the corral was not visible from the house or the fields. "The name's Cole Bradhurst. Don't mean to intrude when you're busy, but I was huntin' . . ." He gestured to a mule deer slung across the back of his horse. "I was huntin' right there on the other side of the river, and I had to come through your farm on my way back to the ranch. Thought I'd stop by and introduce myself."

Elijah extended a hand. Given the isolation along the frontier, visitors—especially unarmed visitors—were generally welcome. "Elijah Norton's my name. Glad to meet ya. You look like you've been in the sun a long time today."

"That is the case, sir."

"Well, my wife, Rachel, she has a drink she makes from fresh raspberries and lime juice, lots of sugar and fresh mint. I believe she's got a jug coolin' in the river, so if you're thirsty, which I expect you are . . ."

Cole untied the red bandanna around his neck and used it to wipe a face that worked well for him. His hair was the color of ripened wheat, and the freckles running beneath his eyes, though faint, were plainly visible. Beneath a firm brow, his eyes were the pure blue of the eastern sky in the afternoon, his nose and mouth small and unobtrusive. He seemed much younger, at first glance, than his forty-two years. Much younger and much more innocent.

"I believe I would, Mr. Norton . . ."

"Elijah, please."

"Okay, Elijah, and call me Cole. But say, why don't I give you a hand with this post. We'd get the job done, and both of us can rest easy."

Elijah held a hatchet in one hand. He'd been about the business of replacing a rotted post, which meant sharpening one end of the new post before hammering it into the ground. The wood planks he'd removed beforehand, too warped for any other use beyond firewood, lay scattered about.

"No need."

But Cole wasn't taking no for an answer. "My daddy was a cabinetmaker in Charleston before the war," he declared. "Seems like another world now, that world before the war. A world gone forever. The Yankees shelled Charleston for 583 days without a letup, and what was left when they finally stopped didn't include my daddy or his workshop."

Cole took the hatchet and tested its edge before he spoke again, his voice soft, entirely without emotion. "Now, my daddy only used the finest wood—mahogany, satinwood, rosewood, tiger maple. And his specialty was inlays of ivory, ebony, marble, and mother-of-pearl. Planters all through South Carolina lined up to buy the furniture he created. It was a beautiful thing to see, the richest planters standing in daddy's workshop, hat in hand. But you couldn't make my daddy rush his work, not usually, although many tried."

"Not usually?" Elijah said, his attention caught.

"Well, some men out there can't be refused. For one example, maybe two years before the war, Governor Jubal Knowles came callin'. Ol' Jubal, as he was known to the votin' public, was the most powerful man in South Carolina. He controlled half the port of Charleston and grew more bright-leaf tobacco than any planter in Charleston County." Cole dropped to a knee and began to work on the new post, slicing off chips of wood with each fall of the hatchet. "Well, seems like the governor's daughter was gettin' married in three months, and he wanted to present her with a bedroom suite as a wedding gift, a job that should take closer to nine months. I'll say this for Jubal Knowles, he brought enough gold with him to pay for three bedrooms. And my daddy took that gold, said thank you, and finished the work two weeks early. Flame birch, if I remember. The chest fronts and tops had veneers of flame birch."

Elijah straightened up. "Mister," he said, "I enjoy the story, and you're doing fine work on that post, but I believe you need to get to the point."

"Only, sir, that there are times in life when we have to put our principles to the side, times when the pressures of life dictate a course of action that can't be resisted." Cole worked on the post for another minute before handing it over. Then he rose to his feet. "It's about your ford, Elijah, the only crossing within

3

sixty miles of where we stand. It's about a rich man with bags of gold waitin' to pay whatever price you ask. Now this rich man, he didn't send me. No, I just happened to be passin', like I said, and thought I'd take the opportunity to alert you. Because this rich man, he sees himself gettin' richer. Fact, that's the only thing he does see, himself gettin' richer, and this here crossing of the Pecos River is how he plans to accomplish that aim. He wants to run his steers on both sides of the river. Him and nobody else."

"Tell me your name again," Elijah demanded. The Norton family had come to the Pecos at a time when the Comanches and Apaches were still in control. Despite numerous raids, they hadn't been driven off, and Elijah wasn't about to be driven off now. He wasn't going to sell out, either. The graves of his father, mother, and sister lay side by side atop a knoll beside the river. Elijah had dug the last two himself, lowered the bodies down, filled in the graves, and chiseled their names into the wooden planks that marked them. That counted for a lot more than a rancher's bag of gold.

"Cole Bradhurst."

"Well, Mr. Bradhurst, take a look around." He gestured to the fields of alfalfa and the acreage given over to fresh produce. Then he pointed in the opposite direction, toward the scrubland on the other side of the river. "When my father brought his wife here forty years ago, the land was the same on both sides. Now you want me to put a dollar price on the blood and sweat he put into buildin' this farm. I'm afraid I can't count that high. Not enough fingers and toes."

Elijah hefted the post, walked it a few steps, and dropped it into the hole left by the rotted post. In doing so, he turned his back on Cole. For his part, Cole didn't hesitate. He held the haft of the hatchet tight in his hand, took a step over the planks ahead of him, and slammed the hatchet into Elijah Norton's head. Cole was surprised when Elijah let out a yell, his voice loud enough to be heard at a distance. The man's skull was depressed a good two inches, the bone smashed and pushed back into his brain. He shouldn't have been able to cry out at all, but there it was.

Cole lifted his eyes to stare fixedly at the side of the barn. There was a house on the other side. Norton's wife and their infant child lived in that house. It wouldn't pay, he told himself, to charge the house, no more than it paid for General Pickett to charge Cemetery Hill at Gettysburg. The woman was, after all, a frontier wife. She might be sitting in a window, shotgun in hand, prepared to defend her child. But if he waited patiently, she was sure to respond to her husband's cry, to seek him out. In the open, of course, she'd be no match for Cole Bradhurst.

But Cole didn't wait. For reasons he was unprepared to consider, he mounted his horse and re-crossed the Pecos River, turning downstream once he reached the other side. A few minutes later, he was out of sight.

CHAPTER 2

Reverend Joshua Hill paused long enough to wipe his forehead with his shirtsleeve, which was a waste of time, as his clothing, from the checkered bandanna around his neck to the darned socks inside his boots, were saturated with sweat. This was West Texas in July, and the temperature was already touching ninety degrees, though noon was still an hour away. Josh looked to the east, along the only street in Whitegrass, past the Pecos River and the flatlands.

Every summer, the baked scrubland drew moisture from the Gulf of Mexico and deposited it in the western deserts. Texas, Arizona, and New Mexico all got their share of the violent thunderstorms that swept across the region, pounding the dry earth with lightning-streaked rain. Arroyos filled in minutes, and placid mountain streams became torrents powerful enough to lift the homes of unwary settlers off their foundations.

"Say, Reverend, you think you could tear yourself away from whatever godly thoughts are runnin' through your head long enough to unload this wagon?"

Josh stood tall and straight, his wide shoulders back. He looked up at the man standing inside the freight wagon, one of two that had rolled into the town of Whitegrass earlier that morning. The loaded wagons had come from San Antonio in formation, a guard cradling a shotgun next to the teamster driver in each wagon, another riding the tailgate in back. There were no towns between San Antonio and Whitegrass, only a few scattered farmers desperate enough to risk the arrival of a Comanche war party after their horses and children. Just two years before, an attack on a wagon train at Howard's Well by Kiowas had resulted in the deaths of twenty travelers, most of them burned alive.

"You in a hurry?" Josh asked the man he knew as Skeeter.

"It happens that I am, Reverend. I'm lookin' to reach Fort Baxter before sunset. There's this little Mexican gal . . ." Skeeter left it there, his words transforming into a laugh that pulled at the leathery skin stretched across his face and neck, turning up an ocean of ripples. Skeeter drove for a company based in Dallas, Badlands Freight System. The company's motto, painted in red on both sides of their wagons, was simple: WE GO WHERE OTHERS CAN'T.

Josh didn't take offense. He did, however, turn away from the smell of alcohol on the man's breath as he hefted a half-barrel of flour. Then he paused for a moment to allow the barrel's ninety-eight pounds to settle in his arms before laying it on its side and rolling it into Whitegrass Mercantile, the general store he ran with his wife, Sarah.

Sarah was standing at the far end of the store, tending to Mary Ellen Granger, the wife to the town's only lawyer. Both women wore hand-sewn gingham dresses. Although partially covered by a muslin counter apron, Sarah's dress—Texas bluebells printed onto a rose-pink base—was especially pleasing to her husband. The dress, form-fitting to the waist, flared over her hips before dropping to within a few inches of the floor.

Josh rolled the barrel into the corner of the store reserved for whatever food couldn't be grown locally. Coffee beans, oatmeal, sugar, dried fruit, molasses, hard candy, and lots of tobacco—the list went on and on. Whitegrass Mercantile was a general store. To Sarah and Josh, that meant generally having whatever their customers needed. Intermittent deliveries, along with the occasional lost cargo, made that job even more challenging. You could telegraph your orders to suppliers in a few seconds, but when you finally received delivery weeks later, you found that much of what you requested had been held back.

"Good morning, Reverend," Mary Ellen called. A stout woman, kind-hearted to a fault, Mary Ellen attended services with her three children every Sunday. Josh only wished the same could be said for her husband. "Did that lace I asked about come in?"

Luxury was difficult to come by on the frontier, and small items could make a big difference to women who endured many privations. Like a bit of lace to trim a hat, the collar of a dress, or the bodice of a shirtwaist.

Josh turned the barrel upright. "Haven't seen it yet, Mary Ellen, but I've still got a ways to go."

"Well, keep an eye out for me."

"Will do." Josh headed back outside to where Skeeter had pushed a wooden crate filled with bottles of medicine packed in straw to the edge of the wagon.

"This is it," Skeeter told him.

"You sure?" Josh asked. "Because I got a telegram yesterday with a list of the supplies supposed to be on this wagon, and it appears there's a crate missing."

"Been through the wagon, Reverend. This here is the whole shebang."

Josh stepped back, shaking his head. Freight wagons were simple affairs, a pair of axles attached to a single rail with a wooden box that resembled a lidless coffin bolted to the top. The greatest variation was in size, and this wagon was huge. Thirty feet long, its red wheels rose to the top of Josh's head.

Far from intimidated by the size of the loaded wagon or the gun tucked into a holster lying against the teamster's hip, Josh pulled himself onto the wagon, his movements surprisingly quick and graceful for a man of his size. On board, he towered over Skeeter, who barely cleared five and a half feet.

"You don't mind, Skeeter, I think I'll take a look around."

The teamster had a choice at that point. He could step back, or he could draw his weapon. He chose to step aside, even though Josh was unarmed.

Josh took his time sifting through the stacked crates, working steadily, never doubting what he'd find in the end. The wagon carried supplies bound for almost every business in Whitegrass—leather for the saddlery, liquor for the Bright Chance Hotel and the Red River Saloon, burlap bags filled with oats for the feed store and the stable, plows for the hardware store, printed forms for the land office, iron for the blacksmith, even supplies for Charlie Drake's lumberyard on the outskirts of town.

Another man would have become discouraged, maybe given up altogether. Not Reverend Joshua Hill. Patience wasn't natural to him. He'd learned patience, as he'd learned to follow the teachings of the Good Book, and he considered both to be great accomplishments. Shifting cargo under a white-hot July sun was the kind of test he welcomed, proof that his wilderness conversion wasn't only the result of the suffering he'd endured.

Josh finally discovered the missing crate behind a long table destined for the dining room of Uriah Thorpe, the wealthiest rancher in Pecos County. Thorpe had come to Whitegrass from Nebraska in 1866, right after the war, bringing Eastern money with him. He'd also brought a young wife, Annabelle, accustomed to the luxuries she had enjoyed back in Omaha. Most folks this far out on the frontier purchased only what they couldn't make themselves.

"Musta got put there when the wagon was loaded," Skeeter muttered. "Don't know nothin' about it."

Josh nodded as he jumped to the ground and slid the box onto his shoulder. There was a time, and not long ago, when he'd clung hard to the belief that every slight had to be answered. He'd carried that belief from childhood into the Civil War and all through his wandering afterward. No more.

"Skeeter, do you believe in God?" Josh asked.

"Course I do."

"Do you believe in Comanches?"

"What kinda fool question . . ."

Josh didn't wait for the teamster to complete the sentence. "Because should a wandering Comanche put an arrow through your heart on the way to Fort Baxter, I'm wondering exactly what you'll tell the God you believe in when you and He are face-to-face."

CHAPTER 3

Josh hauled the crate into the store, relieved to be out of the sun, and freed the nails holding the top in place. "I believe I've got that lace you asked about," he told Mrs. Granger.

"Where'd you find it, Josh?" Sarah asked.

"Behind a table headed for Annabelle Thorpe's dining room."

Mary Ellen's face lit up. "A table? How many does it seat?"

"I'm no expert on dining rooms, Mary Ellen. I'd put the number at eight, but I think it came with an extension." Josh knew exactly what the woman wanted to hear. The women in Whitegrass may have learned how to live without frills, but they still knew how to dream. Josh and Sarah had lived in Whitegrass for three years, and both thought it to be a place of grand ambitions. "I believe the table's made of mahogany. It's rounded at the corners, scalloped along the apron, and the color of South Carolina molasses. Label says it came from Chicago, but I saw tables like it in Virginia. Back before the war."

Josh finally opened the crate, finding the lace and ribbons on top, with two spools of wrapping twine and a sack of table salt below. He picked up the lace and carried it toward the door where the light was strong. The lace he'd received last time out had been off color, slightly yellow, and it had begun to unravel almost before it was sewn onto a garment. Eventually, he'd refunded every dime to his customers, an experience he was not anxious to repeat.

But not this time. Josh discovered a number of patterns, including bellflowers, starbursts, and a bolt that featured a wide field of tiny flowers with a pale blue ribbon at the border. Every inch was exceptionally fine, and he walked back toward the store's counter and Mary Ellen Granger.

Josh found preaching to be a fine occupation, but it didn't pay the bills. That was a good thing, in his opinion. It kept him from confusing the issue. His livelihood didn't depend on pleasing the small congregation that gathered in his even smaller church on the Sabbath. On Sunday mornings, he could look into his heart for inspiration. Meanwhile, Mary Ellen had money to spend.

"Oh, look at this. Isn't it beautiful?" Mary Ellen had fixed her attention on the bolt with the small flowers and the blue ribbon. "I'm cutting the pattern for a new dress. Been at it in my free minutes, which ain't many, Lord knows. This lace would be perfect for the trim."

"We aim to please," Sarah said. Then she looked up at her husband, her blue eyes big enough to pass for waterholes in the desert. "Don't you have business at the church, Josh?"

Josh's smile was genuine enough, but his tone when he responded was a touch rueful. "Thank you, darling," he said, "for reminding me."

Back in Virginia, where Josh had spent his childhood years, the Lutheran church he attended with his parents and siblings had hired its own pastors. Hired them and fired them if they failed to please a congregation dominated by a board of elders. As a child, of course, Josh found no fault with this system. But that was before the war, before the Lost Cause, before he'd wandered for years in a hell of his own design. He knew now that a preacher dependent on a congregation to feed his family would be sorely tempted to tell that congregation exactly what it wanted to hear.

Encouraged by his wife, Josh didn't intend to fall into that trap. He and Sarah eked out a living at the store, a living that would expand as Whitegrass hopefully expanded. As for their two-room church, they'd built that with their own hands and made it clear, when they finally opened the doors, that all were welcome.

"There'll be trouble, husband," Sarah had predicted, "down the line."

That line had apparently been crossed, and Josh was off to face the consequences. He left the store and headed for his church across town.

Josh's church, Whitegrass Community Church, was located behind the jail at the far end of the town's single street. Its front door faced the open prairie and a sky that went on forever, not the town with its hustle, its ambitions, its endless striving. This was by design.

"Morning, Reverend," Doc Cassidy called out as Josh approached.

Jolted back into the present, Josh stopped to shake hands with the town's only doctor. Doc was a short man with an oversized belly he tended to cradle with his forearms, as if he was afraid it'd fall to the ground if he let go. His reputation, when it came to curing disease, wasn't all that strong. But having served on a dozen battlefields during the war, he could handle just about any injury that came his way. He also served as the town's coroner and worked with Ruddy Robinson, the town's red-headed furniture maker and self-appointed undertaker. As death from violence or disease was common on the nation's frontiers, Doc and Ruddy rarely lacked for business.

"Dull scalpels, Josh," he complained. "No blades for the saw. I swear . . . No, I take that back. No swearin' in front of Reverend Hill. But the truth is that I'm keepin' my forceps together with spit and string."

"I take it your supplies weren't delivered." Josh thought of Skeeter, of the possibility that Doc's scalpels were destined for resale in Fort Baxter. Well, he wasn't about to search the wagons for the doctor's supplies, but he'd definitely speak to Sheriff Schofield when he got the chance.

"No, sir, and I was assured that they would be." Doc put a match to the cigar clamped between his teeth. "Way it is now, I could use a butter knife instead of a scalpel and get the same result." He shook his head. "Town like this, Josh, it can't stand still. We either make progress or we're goin' out of business."

Josh nodded agreement and continued on, past the Red River Saloon and the cowboys standing outside, past the office Doc shared with Pace Granger, the town lawyer, past a feed store that sold oats to the stable next door and a hardware store that sold plows to the farmers, past the blacksmith who stood by his forge, sweat running the length of his body as he pounded a horseshoe into shape.

Josh stopped only when he found Padre Pilar standing in front of his own church, Mission de Santa María, a Catholic church built fifty years before the first Texans migrated from Louisiana and Arkansas. Here the single street curved around a stone cistern enclosing a spring that produced water even during the driest months.

"*Buenos días*," Padre Pilar called out. He was a round man with a round head topped by a hat with an upturned brim. His tan robe was tight across his shoulders and only reached midcalf, leading Josh to conclude it had come to the priest as a hand-me-down.

Josh and Padre Pilar were on good terms, neither a threat to the other simply because the Mexican and Anglo populations lived separate lives. That was the situation all through the West. Texas, Arizona, New Mexico, California—it didn't matter. The rivalry was intense, with the Mexicans mostly coming out on the losing end.

"Good morning, Padre," Josh returned. "Are you prayin' for rain too?"

Both men chuckled. The Pecos region only received a scant amount of rain each year, with almost all of it in the summer when the Mexican monsoon came through. The storms were beautiful from a distance, but they could also be life threatening to a traveler without shelter, especially when the lightning was accompanied by hail. Despite the threat, the storms played a crucial part in the economics of Pecos County. Farmers near the Pecos irrigated their crops with water drawn from the river, but those farther away, mostly Mexicans, depended on the summer monsoon.

"*Espero y rezo*," Padre Pilar returned. "I wait and pray."

CHAPTER 4

Josh's church was whitewashed and fronted by a covered porch. The porch had been Sarah's idea. It was customary, she insisted, for a pastor to receive worshippers after Sunday service. Most of those greeted were satisfied with a handshake, but others lingered to discuss problems in town or in their personal lives, or just to chat. Exposure to a blazing summer sun discouraged that tradition. People figured, not unreasonably, that it was hot enough inside the church without roasting outside.

The porch allowed for shade, but there'd been a cost. There was no handy forest this far west. The lumber to construct Josh's church, porch included, had been shipped from the Llano River, a hundred and fifty miles away, through a wilderness infested with bandits and Comanche raiding parties. That's why the buildings along Whitegrass's one street were so plain: planks across the front, signs painted directly on the planks, some walls of wood lumber, some of mud brick or stucco, doors on leather hinges, a flat roof—the absolute minimum.

As Josh approached, he found two men taking advantage of the shaded porch—Paul Wilson and Judah Burke, two of the church's elders. An agreeable man by nature, Paul's greatest flaw, in Josh's opinion, was that he mostly tended to agree with Judah on whatever objective Judah embraced. Judah, for his part, had a sour disposition, like he had been born with a toothache that never went away. Like he wouldn't have that tooth pulled because he enjoyed the pain.

Judah stepped up onto the porch. He started to speak, only to be distracted by a rumble in the distance, a rumble that could only be thunder. He turned, even as the two men glanced past him. Off in the distance, a good thirty miles away, a cluster of gray clouds streaked with charcoal drew together and became one. Then, in an instant, as Josh watched, the cloud descended to the earth, a dancing, swirling veil that was only too welcomed. The storm was too far away for the men on Josh's porch to see the rain hit the ground. But they surely felt it. After months of unrelieved desert sun, any rain seemed miraculous. Josh glanced back along the town's single street. Half the town was outside, eyes shaded, staring off into the distance.

"They'll be complaining soon enough," Judah said.

Judah continued to watch as lightning strikes exploded from the clouds—one, two, then a dozen. The storms would be much larger as the days passed, but they'd not have the same awesome effect. The waiting was over.

Finally, Josh turned to the business at hand. "Complaining about what, Judah?"

"The muddy roads, the flooding. Might not get another freight wagon into Whitegrass 'til fall. That won't be a problem once the Southern-Pacific railroad comes through, assumin' they decide to put a station here."

Near sixty, Judah Burke's height topped six feet by a good five inches. But time had taken its toll, and his broad back was bent at the shoulders. Now he leaned over whomever he happened to be addressing, a deliberate effect that took getting used to, especially for the town's women. He tried the same tactic on Josh that afternoon, but the preacher wasn't intimidated. He looked up at Judah, his eyes fixed on a long-healed scar that ran from Judah's left ear onto his cheek. Judah claimed the scar to be the result of a musket ball fired his way at Second Manassas, but the scar was too thin, at least in Josh's opinion. No, more than likely, it had been caused by a knife. But that was the beauty of life on the frontier. You could erase your past. You could be anything you wanted to be.

"Okay, Judah, what's so important that I had to leave my store?" Josh finally asked.

"We come to you about that . . . that Mexican woman you're shelterin' in our church." Judah's voice was low and raspy. "That heathen's got no business in God's house."

Josh remained stone faced, though he folded his arms across his chest. Judah was wrong, simple as that. Carmelita Mendoza had come to something better. To deny her new station was the same as denying salvation itself.

From the first day, Josh had kept Whitegrass Community Church open to all who wished to attend, including the ladies who worked at the Red River Saloon. Few of these women attended, and fewer still attended regularly, but among those latter was Carmelita, no more than eighteen years old.

Carmelita had appeared every Sunday for months, sitting quietly, head down, barely opening her mouth when hymns were sung. As she rarely spoke to Josh or Sarah on her way out after service, neither of the pair knew whether or not Josh's sermons were having their intended effect. Then, last Sunday, without warning, Carmelita had dropped to her knees and laid her forehead on the rough-hewn planks, her tears flowing so fast they ran along the floor. Her body shook and her sobs poured, not from her mouth, but from her broken heart. No one, not even Sarah or Josh, stepped in to comfort the girl. Carmelita was reaching out to Jesus, and both knew that His hand was already laid upon her shoulder. They simply waited.

When Carmelita finally came back to herself and raised her head, Josh knew she'd taken the Lord into her heart. He'd looked at Sarah, who nodded. There was no sending the girl back to the Red River Saloon. They first offered Carmelita their home, but she wouldn't accept, not even on a temporary basis. Josh then offered the storeroom at the church, explaining that she couldn't very well live out of doors, not in West Texas in the summer. Finally, Carmelita consented, but only until she could find work.

"Judah," Josh finally said, "if Carmelita has no business in the church, where does she have business? If she's turned out, where will she go?"

"Back to her own people. She's a Mexican, and there's a Mexican church not two hundred yards from here." Judah's mouth twisted into a smile so ugly that Josh flinched. "In case you ain't heard, Reverend, white folks and Mexicans don't mix. We got our lives, and they got theirs."

Before he found religion, Josh was known to have somewhat of a temper. He could feel that temper build, feel it burn behind his eyes. But times were different now. Josh understood that anger only put him on a path that led, in the end, to sorrow and its constant companion, despair. He'd abandoned that path when he took up the cloth and was happier for it. Nevertheless, when he spoke out, his tone was cold enough for Judah to take notice.

"You seem a bit lacking in charity, Judah."

"Never you mind, Reverend. It wasn't me who invented hell."

"And it's not your business to put anyone in it." Josh turned away for a moment, reminding himself that Judah also had a soul. He stared off into the distance, surprised to find the storm now little more than a few wispy clouds. Still, despite the storm's brevity, the trees and brush and cactus that lay beneath would throw up flowers within days. Texas persimmon, blue sage, hackberry, sotol. A blanket of butter-yellow flowers would cover the branches of the scattered acacia, and the bunched white brush would resemble snowbanks in the desert. This was another miracle Josh understood to be a gift.

"The Lord didn't come to redeem a select few," Josh finally said, returning to Judah. "He didn't suffer on that cross to save the deserving, either. Jesus came for all mankind, and I have no choice except to follow His example. Carmelita's been saved. As of this moment, her soul is as pure as mine . . . or yours, Judah."

"Speak for yourself, Reverend. As for myself, if there was another white church in Whitegrass, I'd be attending it."

CHAPTER 5

Soon after his own conversion, Josh had been struck by a curious observation. Many of the men and women he met—individuals who believed themselves to be good Christians—held Jesus in their minds instead of their hearts. It was a matter he'd preached on from time to time, generally to little or no effect. Nevertheless, he understood their unshakeable belief in their own salvation to be a lie invented by the greatest liar of all, the human brain. Yet, men still clung to the conviction that words were enough.

"Judah," Josh said, "where and how you worship is your business. But when it comes to running my church, I'm going to listen to my conscience. Carmelita Mendoza has found a lighted path in her troubled life, and I will not send her back into the darkness. As for her moving to Padre Pilar's church, her own church as you might put it, she's welcome to, if that's what she wants. I never asked Carmelita why she chose the Whitegrass Community Church. Any more than I asked the Lord why He chose Carmelita. As a servant of the Lord, I'm satisfied with the result."

The two men stood there for a moment, face-to-face, neither willing to turn away. Then Paul Wilson, who'd been quiet, finally spoke. Paul was small and round, with a droopy gray mustache he combed with his fingers when he was nervous, which he clearly was at that moment. Generally agreeable, he and Judah were partners in a feed store that had recently branched out to include bridles, chaps, and saddles. Whitegrass had a saddle-maker, a Mexican who turned out hand-dyed, hand-tooled saddles that were a sight to behold. They were also too expensive for the cowhands who worked the region's many ranches. By contrast, the

J&P Feed Store's saddles, sold by Judah and Paul, were plain affairs. Imported all the way from Chicago where most of the nation's cattle were slaughtered, they were much cheaper than anything locally produced, yet equally durable.

Life was no different at Whitegrass Mercantile. Ranchers like Uriah Thorpe, who controlled many thousands of acres on the open range, bought supplies at the store, and their hands did as well. The town's local farmers were equally dependent on the big ranchers. Dried and baled, the alfalfa that farmers grew in spring and summer became the hay fed to ranchers' horses in winter.

"It ain't just that woman," Paul said. "No, it's more than that, much more. This here is about survival, Reverend. For the town and every man, woman, or child in it. Had me a visitor the other day, man name of Curtis North. North works for the Southern-Pacific. He's a kind of scout." Paul wore his usual vested gray suit, despite the heat, and his everyday bowler hat. He took off the hat long enough to run a checkered handkerchief over his balding head. "North claims the railroad depots west of the Llano River will be named soon. This far west, he says it's gonna be White-grass or Fort Baxter, one or t'other. Reverend, it's just gotta be us. If not, this town's gonna wither away, like hundreds of other towns stretchin' from here to the Wyoming border. Everything, Reverend, we'll lose everything. And that includes your church and your store."

Josh couldn't argue the point, which the Union-Pacific had already proven correct. Towns skipped by the railroad quickly faded away, while stations and depots prospered.

"What does this have to do with Carmelita Mendoza?" he asked, genuinely puzzled.

Wilson pointed to the Red River Saloon. The four men in front had been joined by one of the women who worked inside. She wore a dress that fell only to her knees, and her bodice was cut deep. Josh watched her laugh at something one of the men said before sidling up next to another.

"Those men—I won't say nothin' about that woman—are drifters. They ain't lookin' for work and wouldn't take work if it was offered to 'em. It's my belief that the one there on left broke into our feed store couple weeks ago. *Our* store, Reverend, and cleared out the cash box. That other one there, with the notch on his hat brim, he was in a gunfight inside the saloon maybe a week ago. Now I could go on and on, but I'm figurin' you get the picture. Curtis North, he gets it too, and he's gonna tell his boss that Whitegrass ain't nothin' but a little cow town providin' women, liquor, and gambling to drifters and local ranch hands out to rid themselves of a month's pay. We ain't got it in us to become the next Dodge City. No sir, not when Whitegrass can't even handle its own business."

Josh had once worked for the Union-Pacific railroad and he could attest, from personal knowledge, that Dodge City had more saloon girls, gunslingers, and gamblers per square inch than any of the towns he'd visited, before or since. Josh wasn't about to lay that fact before Paul and Judah. There was something else going on here, but it didn't appear, on first look, to be Reverend Hill's business.

"I still don't see what Carmelita Mendoza has to do with it," Josh said.

That was Judah's cue, and he stepped forward. "It ain't just about her. It's about you lettin' whores worship in a house of God. It's about heathens runnin' around town like they own it. It's about robbers and brazen thieves showin' themselves in broad daylight. We got to make Whitegrass into a town and, I swear, that's what we intend to do. As for Mexican harlots like your little angel, this is white man's country, Reverend. Has been since Texas became a state. East of here, the issue was settled before the war, settled hard. Now it's our turn."

"To do what, Judah?"

"To meet our destiny, as ordained by a different Lord than the one you worship."

Josh had to remind himself, as he watched Judah and Paul stride away, their stiff backs and high chins making their disdain obvious, that he was as obligated to the two men as he was to Carmelita. Still, the words of Matthew rang out, though no voice spoke them aloud: *No man can serve two masters: for either he will hate the one and love the other; or else he will hold to the one and despise the other. Ye cannot serve God and mammon.*

No issue here. In Aramaic, the word mammon simply means money, Aramaic being the language probably spoken by Jesus.

Paul and Judah were supremely ambitious, as were many others on the frontier. To the west, between the Pecos and the Rio Grande, lay the Chihuahuan Desert, last homeland of the Comanche, the Kiowas, and the Apache. The end was coming for the western tribes and everyone knew it, except for those Indians determined to make a last stand. Their cause was hopeless because the railroad, the Southern-Pacific, was already under construction. It would cross that desert within the next ten years, sweeping the tribes before it, leaving riches in its wake, riches for whomever managed to take them.

At least one piece was already in place. The cattle in the trans-Pecos had simply run wild after both armies, Yank and Reb, withdrew from the region. Some estimated there to be tens of thousands of cows and bulls awaiting the branding iron of whichever outfit rounded them up. Men like Uriah Thorpe meant themselves to be among the first, an ambition he wasn't ashamed to state in public.

The greed didn't surprise Josh. The war had left the defeated South literally destitute, Southern money having been declared worthless by the victorious Union. Adding to the misery, there were more widows than women with husbands, and more wives with crippled husbands than whole. Some men collapsed under the weight of their troubles. Suicides were an everyday occurrence. But others—especially the young—left their devastated homes in search of something, anything, better. They took their ambitions with them, of course, along with their desperation. Josh knew this because he'd been one of them.

Josh's thoughts were interrupted by hoofbeats. He turned to find a horse and rider coming toward him at a steady gallop. The rider wore a duster and his hat was pulled low over his head, but Josh recognized the roan gelding he rode as belonging to Deputy Sheriff Hank Potter. Josh knew Hank to be especially fond of the animal, but the horse—its shoulders and flanks whitened with lather—had been hard used. Whatever the deputy was about, it had to be serious.

Josh expected Hank to pass by on his way to the sheriff's office and the jail, but he pulled to a halt in front of the church.

"Reverend," he said, "we got us some trouble out at Elijah Norton's place."

"What kind of trouble?" Josh's heart froze in his chest. He and Sarah had been friends with Elijah and his wife, Rachel, almost from the day Josh and Sarah arrived in Whitegrass. They'd shared meals together, and Josh and Sarah had stood as godparents to the Nortons' only child—six-month-old Eli.

Deputy Potter wore a hat with a broad, floppy brim. He pulled the sweat-soaked hat off his head and slapped it against his thigh, sending off a little shower of droplets. "Elijah was attacked, Reverend, and his skull's broken. Don't look like he's gonna make it. Rachel asked me to fetch you. She's hopin' you'll say a few words before his passin'. I'm going now to fetch Doc Cassidy."

There it was, simple in the western way, in the way of men and women dwelling in a dangerous land, trouble always close at hand. Josh's answer, when he responded, was equally simple.

"Do me a favor, Hank. After you get the doc, stop by the store and tell Sarah where I went."

"I will surely do that, Reverend."

CHAPTER 6

Cole Bradhurst, although exhausted from three long days on the open range, and from what he'd done at the end of the expedition, knew better than to sit on any of the dozen chairs in Uriah Thorpe's great room. That's what the man called it: his great room. Well, the room was definitely big. Cole conceded that much as he stood before his employer. Too big, by a wide margin, for the three people inside, though not for the display of Thorpe's mighty-hunter credentials.

Thorpe's collection of dead animals—heads and skin from a Montana grizzly bear, to an Eastern moose shot in Maine, to a pronghorn taken on the ranch—blanketed the walls and floors. Two stuffed gray wolves at the center of the room, their intent eyes focused directly forward, seemed all but on the prowl. Before the fieldstone fireplace at the far end of the room, the skin of a diamondback rattlesnake stretched to a length of eight feet. Even so, it didn't come near matching the width of the hearth behind it.

Cole no longer wore his plain shirt and Levis or his worn vest. He'd changed into a silk shirt, red with a faint gray stripe, and black twill trousers of the type called Edgars. His elaborately quarter-stitched boots gleamed, even in the dim, late-afternoon light filtering through the open windows, as did the mother-of-pearl grips on the Colt Peacemaker strapped to his thigh.

Uriah spoke first, though he let Cole stand there for an awkward moment. The rancher turned to his wife, Annabelle, and said, "I need to have a private word with Cole. If you don't mind."

Cole smiled to himself. Uriah and he might easily have had this word in another room, or even outside. Instead, he was ordering his wife to lay her teacup aside and vacate the room. Annabelle knew it too, though she seemed more amused than offended. Before rising, she flicked a plainly invitational glance in Cole's direction. Cole didn't acknowledge the glance—he never did—though he had to admit the woman, with her dark red hair and pale skin, was truly beautiful.

On her feet, Annabelle took a few seconds to smooth the pleats on her slate-gray dress, before moving past Cole and out of the room. Though graceful, her walk, like everything else about her, seemed carefully controlled, including a second alluring glance, this one more than casual.

"Well?" Uriah said once his wife was out of earshot. "Did you do it?"

"Norton's taken care of."

"What about the woman?"

"Do you mean Norton's wife, Mr. Thorpe?"

"There's no other woman out there."

Cole hesitated. He was tempted to say that he'd looked for her in the house, but he couldn't bring himself to lie to Uriah, a man he despised. "I left her to care for her child," he finally said.

"And you're what then? A man of compassion? A humanitarian?"

"No, sir, but . . ."

"But what?"

Cole found himself unable to come up with an answer that would satisfy either his employer or himself. He'd spent most of the war defending his hometown of Charleston, South Carolina, an important port town of the Confederacy. He had watched a proud city reduced to rubble, lived through bombardment after bombardment, weeks and months of daily shelling. Shells don't discriminate. They do not separate women, children, and the elderly from uniformed personnel. This lesson had been driven home every time Cole and his company sifted through the rubble after a barrage, lifting out the bodies. Those images still haunted his dreams, one especially. His company had lifted a section of wall to find, beneath it, a young woman cradling an infant to her breast, their bodies so smashed they might have been a single object.

"I don't believe our understanding," Cole finally said, "requires me to kill women and children."

Cole endured his boss's hard stare. He wasn't about to speak first, more afraid of losing his temper than offending the man. Uriah Thorpe's entire life was devoted to intimidation. He lived to dominate, using his height and weight, his words, and his money to achieve that end. Yet he'd sent another man to do his killing when he might easily have done it himself. Might have done it himself and left no one to bear witness.

"So, that's it? No women, no children, only helpless farmers?" Uriah's mocking laughter echoed in the room. But then he looked into Cole's eyes and his laughter died away. He'd made a mistake with Cole, assuming the man to be ruthless, assuming him to be solely motivated by money. Take the job, do the work. That wasn't the case, obviously, and Uriah could only hope that the man wasn't, at bottom, crazy as a loon.

"I'm sure you know," Uriah continued, "what the Comanches do to women and children. And what the American cavalry does to the Comanches and any other Indians they catch in camp, regardless of age and gender. Seems like you're behind the times, Cole."

"I have no opinion about the times, or about what other men do. But I just couldn't leave that baby an orphan."

"Then you should have killed the baby, too."

CHAPTER 7

Josh, after receiving the news from the deputy, headed directly to the stables where Faro Lamb, the owner, helped him saddle a dun mare with a dark mane that Josh and Sarah had named Sunset. Never fast to begin with, Sunset was aging but steady. She'd run all day if Josh demanded the effort. But the last thing he needed was for the beast to collapse halfway to the Norton farm, so he headed off at a slow but steady cantor.

The road he took was closer to a trail than the roads he had known back East in Virginia. Every strike of Sunset's hooves threw up a cloud of dust that hung in the still air, splitting the sun's rays into a million parts. Josh was cautious enough to toss an occasional glance over his shoulder—whoever attacked Elijah might be still around—but his thoughts drifted as he continued on.

Off to his right, the banks of the Pecos were lined with trees and brush, their green leaves contrasting sharply with the browned scrub to the west. The river itself was out of sight between its banks, and Josh was instantly reminded of Shiloh and the Hornet's Nest. The Yanks had set up a defensive line on a sunken road and they were dug in hard enough to repel attack after attack. It wasn't until late afternoon, when the Rebels took a knoll above the road, that the tide turned—a tide of blood as it turned out. The Confederates were able to fire down onto the road, fire at will, almost every shot finding flesh.

Only a few months later, Josh watched the same scene unfold at Antietam, only this time reversed, with Rebel defenders packed together like sardines in a can, maybe the worst thing they could have done. Every musket ball fired from the Union position seemed to draw blood.

Josh wasn't in the road at either battle. He'd been a way off, still in the fighting but in a protected position and relatively safe. And so, he'd watched as the hours passed, the bodies piled up, and the blood pooled in every crevice. At times the artillery fire had been continual, a single explosion, a single flash of flame and smoke that went on and on until the soldiers beneath those deadly shells preferred the gates of hell to another minute under the barrage.

But there was no escape while the war continued, and Josh had followed a trail that ran from one hell to another, one battle to another, from First Manassas to Fredericksburg to Vicksburg, all the way to Appomattox, until he saw, whenever he closed his eyes, piles of amputated limbs awaiting a burial of their own, until he heard in the quiet of the early morning, not the call of the awakened birds, but the screams of the maimed and dying.

He'd carried that memory with him after the war, a man of violence accepting jobs that required violence—first as an enforcer for the Union-Pacific, then as a hired gun in two range wars, the Colfax County War in New Mexico and the Lee-Peacock Feud, then as the marshal in the mining town of Railford, where he acted solely in the interests of the Jubilee Mining Association. Josh put down no roots at any of these stops, took no wife, built no home, so he never had a reason to stay, and after a time he became lost to himself and to the world. He wandered in the wilderness, the great canyons of Arizona where the rising sun turned the cliffs into castles of gold, the Nebraska prairie amid herds of buffalo that appeared to be a single shaggy beast, its body rippling as its cropped grasses swayed in time to a perennial wind, the Rocky Mountains where snowcapped peaks spoke of worlds hidden from the eyes of men.

Finally, in 1868, in early spring, for no reason beyond his reluctance to tolerate the company of other human beings, he found himself in Montana, in the foothills of the Bitterroot, when his horse stepped into a hole and broke its leg. A man of long experience, Josh should have known better, yet found himself unprepared to be on foot in what was still a wilderness. This early in the year, any plants he might have eaten were no more than green buttons pushing through the newly thawed earth. There were deer to be had, but they were half-starved after the long winter, reduced to bone and dry muscle, fat reserves totally exhausted. He tried to fish at one point, but the streams were foaming torrents of meltwater and cold enough to instantly numb his flesh.

Time was not on his side. The nights were still bitter cold and the days only a bit warmer. It snowed hard on the second night, which made every step a chore, but there was no way out except by walking. Much of that walking was uphill, but the effort it took wasn't the worst of it. The worst was reaching the top of a hill and finding nothing ahead of him but the forest and the howling wind.

Josh didn't notice at first, but as his strength and his will faded, exposing his naked soul, the knot of despair that tore at his bowels, that pulled every dream from his heart, began to loosen. How long did it take before his bonds fell away? Weeks, surely, until one afternoon, while the sun was still up, he made a fire and lay down next to it, too tired to move, resigned to his fate.

The sky was clear, the moon bright enough that night to throw shadows across the snow. Josh watched a shooting star fly past the other stars, coming straight for him, and he called out to his Creator for the first time, not for help, but for something he could not name.

He woke up the next morning to voices. A wagon train on its way to California's central valley had come across his footprints in the snow and dispatched a search party. In their company, Josh found the energy to ride the horse they brought, but when he finally reached the line of wagons snaking their way through a twisting valley, he collapsed. Anxious to keep moving, the wagon master loaded Josh onto a Conestoga wagon belonging to Horst Danielson and his widowed daughter, Sarah. That night, in addition to bowls of prairie-chicken soup, Sarah had placed a worn Bible in her patient's hand. Josh took the book from Sarah and placed it in his heart. Not long after, he found a bit more room for Sarah herself, a woman he'd come to love more than his own life.

Josh could still recall the wedding, performed by the Reverend Wallace Friend, a preacher on his way to Sacramento, there to join . . .

Josh tilted his head up as the Norton farm came into view. The effect, as always, was startling, the dull-brown scrub giving way to a field of bright-green alfalfa, the dividing line ruler straight. Alfalfa was a two-crop plant, and the early crop was beginning to flower and ready for harvest. Elijah had visited Whitegrass in search of field workers twice in the past two weeks. Each time, he'd met with Padre Pilar, hoping to find workers in the Mexican community who could wield a scythe. The local cowboys thought farm work of any kind beneath them.

If it could be successfully cut and baled, the Nortons' alfalfa would be sold to local ranchers. If not, the farm would almost surely be lost. Grieving or not, Rachel would have to deal with this reality. The crop wouldn't wait on her.

Josh rode into Elijah Norton's front yard to find Sheriff Trey Schofield standing on the porch of Elijah's three-room house. Only a few feet away, handcuffed to a railing, the Nortons' single field hand, Francisco Rivera, sat with his head bent, staring at his feet. Blood was plainly visible on his hands and his clothing. Josh examined the man as he dismounted and tied Sunset to a hitching post. Francisco had only been with the Nortons for a couple of weeks, but Elijah had praised the man as a diligent and tireless worker.

"Bad day, Josh," Schofield said as he descended the porch steps to grip Josh's hand. Schofield had been a Texas Ranger almost from the day Texas came into existence. Over the years, he'd dealt with every kind of horror one human can inflict on another, and he'd done it without flinching. Not this time. The sheriff's features had pulled in on themselves, and his face was one of a man who'd seen too much undeserved death. Maybe it was the badly broken nose, flattened and bent to the left, or the worn star, dust covered, that hung from his leather vest. "You better get inside. Elijah's pretty near gone."

Although a thousand questions tumbled through his mind, Josh marched into the house, through a sitting room with a cooking stove at one end. All the furniture in the room had been made by Elijah or his father, who'd come to the Pecos before the war, including the rocking chair reserved for Rachel throughout her pregnancy. The same held true in the bedroom where Elijah lay. The bedstead, the two small chests, and a freestanding clothes closet had been crafted by Elijah or his father. Only a hope chest at the foot of the bed with its hand-painted vines and flowers broke the pattern. Rachel had carried the chest all the way from Pennsylvania.

You don't spend as many years engaged in war as Josh Hill and not know when death is imminent. Even beyond the ragged wound at the back of his head, Elijah's skin was the white of flour in a barrel, and his eyes, though open, were barely focused until he saw Josh. Then he looked past his sobbing wife, into Josh's eyes, and asked a question without speaking.

Josh stepped forward to lay his hand on Elijah's shoulder. "We'll see to Rachel and the baby," he promised. "Sarah and me. I give you my word."

Elijah settled down then, his gaze turning inward as he fell into a deep sleep from which, Josh knew, he would not awaken. Josh's first impulse was to join Rachel in her grief. He loved Elijah as he'd once loved his own brother, lost in the war, and he had to close his eyes for a moment to stop the tears.

Josh knelt beside the bed and took Elijah's hand. When Josh did finally speak, his voice was shaky, but still firm enough to be understood.

"Lord, I come to you as your servant. Please forgive me, born as I am of a string of dust, from tellin' You anything. You, who are everywhere. You, who already know the before and after of the world. But a man is comin' your way, a man of good deeds and kind heart, a man by the name of Elijah Norton. He sang Your praises on the Sabbath, Lord, in my presence. And what I could see by only half-lookin' was that the words comin' out of his mouth began their journey in his heart. Now I ask You to look into that heart when it comes time for judgement. I ask You to look past the imperfections that come with the wearing of this corruptible flesh and find a simple man who loved You always. Amen."

Josh remained by the bed with his head bowed and spoke from Psalms: *The Lord is my shepherd; I shall not want. He maketh me to lie down in green pastures. He leadeth me beside the still waters. Yea, though I walk through the valley of the shadow of death, I will fear no evil for thou art with me.*

Josh stood up and stepped back. There was the waiting now, the inevitable death watch. Rachel's tears still flowed freely as she held her husband's hand and lay her head upon his chest. Josh could only stand there, knowing that whatever consolation he had to offer would come later, until Elijah's last breath rattled in his chest. Rachel rose at that point, her sad eyes finally meeting Josh's.

"I can't leave him like this," she said. "I need to wash away the blood."

Josh wanted to comfort her, to take her into his arms as he would a young child, to press her head against his chest, to offer himself as a refuge against the evil that had befallen her. That was impossible, and he couldn't even bring himself to take her hand. Sarah would do the comforting when she arrived. Until then, he could only offer a half-whispered, "I'm so sorry." Then he turned on his heel and walked out of the room.

CHAPTER 8

Josh came out of the house to find Sheriff Schofield standing guard over Francisco. Still handcuffed to the rail, Francisco's stare was fixed on his bloody hands as his lips moved rapidly.

"*Dios te salve, María. Llena eres de gracia . . .*"

Josh nodded, then turned his attention to a bloodstained hatchet lying near the steps. "You wanna tell me what happened?" he asked the sheriff.

Schofield might have told Josh to mind his own business. He might have demanded that Josh tend to Elijah Norton's soul and leave earthly justice to him. But they'd been friends too long.

"This ain't right," Schofield declared. "Elijah never harmed nobody."

Josh responded with a verse from Matthew, though he couldn't number it: "*For He makes His sun rise on the evil and the good, and sends His rain on the just and the unjust.*"

"Can't say I find them sentiments of much comfort, Reverend."

"Comforting or not, they're all we have. They're also true."

Schofield responded with a lopsided smile but made no further argument. Instead, he chose to answer the question Josh first asked. "Had to be two hours after Elijah was attacked before I got here. By then, Francisco and Rachel had moved Elijah from behind the barn into the house. Rachel was close to broke down, as you'd expect with her husband nearly gone, but that made what happened to Elijah a murder. So, I persisted, gentle-like, until I finally got her story."

He turned without another word and led Josh behind the barn. Elijah had built a small corral there for the farm animals, and a section had been removed for some kind of repair. It was lying atop a pair of logs Elijah used as a sawhorse, and there were tools lying about. Right beside those logs, the hard-packed earth was dark with blood that had dried in the sun.

For a long moment, they simply stood there, the preacher and the sheriff, imagining what must have gone down as they listened to the relentless buzz of the hungry flies. Buzzards circled above them, their black wings tipping from side to side as they searched for rising currents of desert air. Unlike the hawks and eagles with their piercing cries, the buzzards were as silent as they were relentless.

"Rachel was in the house," Schofield finally said, "when she heard her husband cry out. She was feedin' little Eli, and it took her some time to put him safe. It seems little Eli didn't like his mealtime bein' interrupted and he put up a fuss."

"How much time?"

"Maybe five minutes, but Rachel wasn't certain, and I didn't press the issue. She didn't hurry, though, because there was only the one cry and she thought it likely that Elijah had uttered some profanity in a moment of frustration. But when she finally got to the corral, there was Francisco, kneelin' over Elijah with a hatchet, bloodstained, right next to his knee."

"What about Elijah? Did Elijah name Francisco?"

"By the time I got to him, Elijah was past talkin'. But Rachel told me that when he woke up for a few minutes, he was the one askin' what happened. The man was hit real hard on the head, Josh, hard enough to push a piece of his skull into his brain. It ain't uncommon for a man to lose his memory after such a blow."

The rattle of approaching wheels interrupted their conversation. Josh and Schofield hurried around the side of the barn to discover Deputy Hank Potter piloting a freight wagon onto the property. Potter nodded to the sheriff as he hopped down, then walked over to Francisco and quickly uncuffed him. Josh knew he couldn't interfere. This was business that belonged to Caesar, not to God. Still, as Josh watched Francisco struggle to rise, he instinctively knew there was trouble ahead, trouble that would draw him in. Francisco, favoring his bad leg, hobbled over to the wagon and climbed aboard. Josh stared at the man, looking for any hint of violence, but Francisco seemed resigned to his fate. Josh had seen that expression—mouth set, eyes lidded, jaw relaxed—on the faces of captured Indians when he worked for the Union-Pacific. They appeared merely to be waiting, almost indifferently, for whatever happened next.

Josh nodded to Deputy Potter but quickly turned back to Sheriff Schofield. "Did you question Francisco?" he asked. "Because him killing Elijah don't seem possible. Why would he stick around until Rachel came out if he had just killed her husband? Why would he help her get Elijah into the house? Why didn't he run off before you got here?"

"I expect it was because he was remorseful. That happens sometimes when the killin' comes by way of an impulse."

"Did he confess?"

Schofield shook his head. "Francisco told me that he was out in the field, near about three hundred yards away on the other side of the barn. He come when he heard Elijah shout, but it took him some time because of his bad leg. Keep in mind, the corral ain't visible from the fields or from the house. But when he did circle the barn, Francisco claims he found Elijah lyin' on his face, not movin'. Naturally, he turned Elijah over, hopin' he could be of some help, and that's how he got the blood on him. The hatchet was just layin' there. According to Francisco, he never touched it."

"But you don't believe him."

"There's flatland all around the farm, Josh. Don't appear like a man could up and vanish before Rachel come out of the house." Schofield hesitated. "Look, I know Francisco doesn't seem like a violent type, and maybe I do have some doubt. But that don't matter. The man has family in Mexico. If he slips across the border, we'll never see him again. I can't take that chance, so what I'm gonna do is lock him up. What with all the circumstances, I got no choice except to let a judge and jury decide the matter."

Josh got the message, though he didn't like it. The sheriff was an elected official and he'd have to run for office in a few months. Now he was protecting his flank, a wartime lesson he'd apparently mastered.

"If you were in town when Elijah was attacked," Josh asked, "how'd you know to ride out here?"

"A cowboy name of Cole Bradhurst, one of Uriah Thorpe's hands."

Josh considered the implications for a moment, then said, "So, this cowboy . . ."

"Cole Bradhurst."

"Yes, Cole Bradhurst. You're saying he forded the river before he came on the scene?"

"Yessir. Claims it was his day off and he was huntin'"

"You don't find that suspicious?"

"He said he crossed the river with the stagecoach that happened to be coming through and followed it all the way into town." Schofield didn't need to elaborate. Travelers in the region often bunched together, a matter of safety in numbers. "And by the way, he had a fresh-killed mule deer slung across the back of his horse, so the huntin' part holds up, too. That don't mean I'm givin' up on Francisco. It's just that for now, I'm makin' sure my suspect stays where I can find him. I owe that to the folks who pay my salary."

With nothing more to say, Schofield nodded once, then mounted his horse. He signaled to his deputy in the wagon and Potter shook the reins, urging his mule into a walk. The sheriff followed without looking back. Not close to satisfied, Josh watched Schofield and the wagon retreat.

There were trials, Josh knew, and then there were fair trials. The evidence presented at Francisco's trial would be heard by an all-white jury, many of whom shared Judah Burke's opinions. They would not be fair. Still, Josh and Sarah had decided, almost upon their arrival, to remove themselves from town politics. They knew they would find many factions in Whitegrass, as Josh had found them in every town he'd visited in the course of his wanderings. Many factions, yet only one teaching, one message, one Lord, and one, single Redeemer. Josh's job, Sarah's too, was to make His Word available to all sides. That couldn't happen if he took up with one side or the other.

Josh's thoughts were interrupted by the sight of his own buckboard coming up fast. Sarah held the reins, with Doc Cassidy beside her. The Hills' mule pulled the wagon, an incredibly stubborn animal named Pharaoh that Sarah could somehow coax into a steady trot. When she came abreast of the sheriff's wagon, Sarah pulled Pharaoh to a halt. Josh couldn't make out her words, but he watched her point to Francisco and shake her head. Apparently unimpressed, Sheriff Schofield doffed his hat before moving on.

A few minutes later, Sarah again pulled to a halt, this time beside her husband.

"Where's Rachel?" she asked. "How's Elijah?"

Josh looked into a pair of eyes streaked with red. Those eyes were now dry, and he knew his wife had sucked back her own feelings. She and Rachel Norton were as close as sisters. "She's in the house, tending Elijah's body. Elijah passed near a half hour ago." He tipped his hat to Doc. "Looks like you wasted your time, Doc."

"I need to examine him anyway. If there's a trial, I'll be asked to establish the cause of death."

Sarah and Josh watched the doctor walk inside, his cane thumping along the porch, before Sarah spoke again. "Did you get here in time?" she asked.

Josh reached up to take his wife's hand and felt her instantly soften. They lived in a hard part of the world, and something always seemed to be pushing at them to respond by hardening themselves. They could resist, but the pushing part never went away.

"I asked the Lord to judge Elijah Norton by the contents of his heart."

Josh stood there until Sarah entered the house, remembering that he'd promised Elijah that they would see to his wife and child. He hadn't asked Sarah beforehand. He didn't have to.

CHAPTER 9

Josh could have hurried back to town. His horse was well rested, and the sun was dropping down behind the ridges far off to the west. The temperature was already falling. It would reach the low seventies by dawn. That would leave only a few hours until the funeral, and there was work aplenty before he had to face Rachel and the other mourners. But he couldn't get the sheriff's words out of his mind. Francisco must have murdered Elijah because . . . What was it Schofield said?

"There's flatland all around the farm. Don't seem like someone could up and vanish before Rachel come out of the house."

Schofield was right. The land on either side of the river barely rolled, and the arroyos were shallow. A rider on horseback would have to travel a long way before he was truly out of sight. There'd be hoofbeats, too, unless he walked his horse, which would have made escape even slower.

Josh again circled the barn, stopping when he stood in the center of the corral. Surely, if you were going to attack someone, this was the place to do it. The corral couldn't be seen from the house or from the fields.

The corral was in shade by that time, and Josh's view was to the east across the Pecos where the sun skimmed over the brush and grass, adding color to everything it touched. Most evenings, Josh took a moment to watch the sun as it dropped below a horizon that seemed as far away as the stars already visible in the eastern sky. Josh tended to see the Lord's hand in the turnings of the world, and he saw it that evening as well—saw the mystery of it and his own helplessness before that mystery.

But the mystery surrounding Elijah's murder was of a different order, and Josh quickly turned his mind back to the relevant circumstances. Elijah's parents had come from Alabama before Elijah's birth. Without meaning to, at least according to Elijah, they had laid claim to a piece of land that included a natural ford of the Pecos River. Compared to mighty rivers like the Mississippi and the Missouri, the Pecos was little more than a stream. At the same time, it was almost impossible to drive a herd of cattle across its waters, as many a foolhardy rancher had learned the hard way. There were patches of quicksand large enough to swallow a steer, and the banks tended to be too steep and muddy to climb. The cattle would bunch at the foot of those banks, with the steers farthest behind unable to clear the river. That forced ranchers driving their herds to use natural crossings like Horsehead Crossing eighty miles north of Whitegrass.

The Nortons, Josh knew, weren't vindictive. They might have charged a fee to cross the river and made a decent living off what amounted to a piece of luck. But they were farmers and neighbors. They allowed riders and wagons, including the passing stagecoaches, to cross their property day or night. And if it had proven possible to drive a herd of cattle or horses through without damaging crops, they would have allowed the herds as well. Unfortunately, Josh thought, both species were intelligent enough to prefer the Nortons' lush alfalfa to the burnt-up grass out on the range. No matter how skilled and diligent the cowboys attending them, the herds would break apart and graze as soon as the animals reached the farm.

Josh walked to the edge of the river and looked into the scrubland on the far side. Outside of the occasional thorny acacia and a few dense patches of prickly pear, there was no cover to be had. By contrast, the land bordering the river on either side was as green as the Virginia meadows where Josh spent his boyhood. The trees were taller and fuller, likewise for the brush. Cottonwood, desert willow, Mexican buckeye, Texas walnut, and a dozen other species competed on two narrow strips, each no more than thirty feet wide. Josh couldn't help but speculate. Was there room to hide a man and a horse inside that growth? More than a few of the big ranchers in the area, including Uriah Thorpe, wanted the crossing open to all, the better to exploit both banks of the river. But others took a more temperate view.

The Southern-Pacific, when it came through in a few years, would cross the Pecos on a bridge. Other bridges would follow, and the issue would resolve itself. In the meantime, the hay grown at the Nortons' farm was the best to be had. The Nortons grew produce as well—corn, pumpkins, squash, and tomatoes, six varieties of beans suitable for drying, blackberries, strawberries, and peaches, even honey from their own hives. They sold this produce in town to grateful customers who did without for much of the year. Despite the summer heat, this part of West Texas didn't support crops year-round. Winters were cold, especially the long nights in January and February when temperatures fell below freezing almost every night.

The sound of his wife's voice ended Josh's speculations. He shook his head and smiled. As a town marshal in Railford, Josh had routinely investigated crimes, including murder. Some habits, he told himself, die hard.

"How's Rachel doing?" he asked as he came into view of the house. Sarah was standing on the porch, her expression grim yet stubborn. As always, she would persevere.

"I don't believe the loss has set in fully, Josh. Something this big, the mind doesn't want to take it in."

"Is there anything I can do?" Josh watched his wife shake her head. "What about Doc Cassidy?"

"He'll borrow one of Elijah's . . . I mean one of Rachel's horses and ride back later." She stopped for a moment to run her hands through her hair. "I'm going to stay the night, maybe tomorrow night too. There's so much to think about, what with the crop needing to be harvested. I'm already seeing flowers on the alfalfa."

Alfalfa, Josh knew, must be harvested before it fully flowered or it lost much of its nutritional value and the ranchers wouldn't buy it. The ranchers wouldn't buy it and there was no one else to sell it to. He stepped onto the porch and kissed his wife. "We'll find the help somewhere. Tell Rachel not to worry."

Sarah held her husband's hand for a moment, then said, "Funny thing, but it's not the crops worrying Rachel. She's worried about Francisco. Claims he's a gentle man by nature and he only took the job so he could send money off to his family in Mexico." Sarah put her hands on her hips, a gesture Josh knew well. She was certain of what she was going to say next. "If Francisco murdered his employer, he'd already be in Mexico. And maybe killed Rachel too, if he was after money. Instead, he helped Rachel bring her husband into the house. Instead, he lit a fire when she asked and boiled the cloths she used to treat her husband's wound. Those are not the actions of a killer."

CHAPTER 10

His wife's thoughts chased Josh all the way back to their home above Whitegrass Mercantile. They stayed with him as he worked his way through his Bible in search of suitable passages for the services he'd conduct on the following day. He found the references easily, drawing some from memory, others from a key that broke biblical passages into categories. From Matthew to Thessalonians to Revelations to Isaiah, the Good Book sought to comfort the grieving, not least because their intense suffering could not be ignored. But what comfort could be given a wife and mother who'd lost her husband, still a young man, to a murderer?

Josh stopped for a moment. Elijah Norton's physical death, he reminded himself, was absolute. Elijah would not return, no matter how fervent the prayers of his wife. If there was comfort to be had, it was in a future, a time, still unknown, when Rachel and Elijah would be reunited. In the meantime, trapped in her own flesh, Rachel would have to continue to meet the demands of the flesh, along with the unceasing demands of her child. Little Eli knew nothing of death, of finality, of a grief that comes near to madness. Helpless as he was, he knew only of his many personal needs.

It was Josh's job to put his own grieving aside and provide Rachel with the strength to go forward. That wouldn't be accomplished in an hour, no matter how persuasive the homily he delivered. She would need support, day to day. That was what humans did, all they could do. There was a crop to harvest. Josh had learned to wield a scythe in Virginia, back before the war, a time when everybody except the big planters pitched in at harvest time. And Sarah could—and would—set up a counter inside Whitegrass Mercantile to sell Rachel's freshly picked fruits and vegetables . . .

Enough, Josh told himself. He could take all the vows in the world, pledge himself and his wife to any kind of service. The proof would be in the doing. In the meantime, his own needs had to be met. He hadn't eaten since lunch and had no desire to fire up the wood stove and prepare a meal. It was full night by that time. The temperature had already fallen ten degrees, and the cool, dry air sifting through his window called out to him. The message was simple enough. The world as it continued to spin was not without its consolations.

On his way out, Josh took a final look around the small space he called home. There wasn't all that much to look at. Half the front room was given over to storage, and the rest, like the Nortons', seemed improvised. With only three exceptions, the furniture had been cobbled together from whatever materials had been available at the time. The exceptions were a camelback settee upholstered in navy-blue wool and a rocking chair crafted from tiger's-eye maple that Sarah polished every week. Both were wedding gifts from Sarah's father, Horst Danielson, who'd cried his eyes out at the wedding. On his way to California, there to join his wife and son, Horst knew there was a good chance that he'd never see his daughter again. Such was life on the country's frontier.

The third exception, also a gift from Horst, was a gilt-framed mirror that hung near the top of the stairway leading to the ground floor. Josh glanced into that mirror as he closed the door. He found a tired man, rapidly approaching middle age, in need of a haircut and a shave. There was an abundance of gray in his dark hair, and thin lines radiated from his eyes and the corners of his mouth. Josh, far from pleased with his reflection, squared his shoulders, raised his chin, and smoothed his hair. Instinctively, he sought refuge in pronouncing himself vain. In truth, he was asking himself a question: Who am I?

***

Josh happened on Smithson Wright, owner of the Bright Chance Hotel, as he entered the hotel lobby. Smitty's story, which he loved to share, was captivating, as he meant it to be. He'd voyaged from the Ohio frontier to California in 1849, a year after gold was discovered at Sutter's Mill. Shrewd by nature, he had made a fortune in the gold fields, gambled it away, made another, and lost that one too. He was past forty by then, his constitution weakened by years of abuse. The business of opening a new mine was beyond him. So, he sold everything he had and headed off to West Texas, where he put the last of his money to use. The chairs in the Bright Chance's lobby were upholstered in Eastern leather, the tables sprinkled throughout of mahogany with a rosewood inlay, and the walls on all four sides covered in kelly-green velvet. Smitty, as he liked to tell it, was investing in the future.

"I know you and Elijah were good friends," Smitty said. "Let me offer my condolences."

"Thank you."

Smitty shook Josh's hand. "Bad business, Reverend. White farmer murdered by a Mexican worker? This ain't good news for anyone."

Josh nodded, having already drawn this conclusion, at least about the trouble part. Still, he was struck by the worry in Smitty's brown eyes. A gambler to his bones, Smitty had sunk every last dime into the hotel.

"We'll be okay," Josh said, "If we keep our heads."

The Bright Chance's dining room reflected the same basic strategy on display in the lobby. Smitty had gone all out to create a real hotel because he believed in the town's future as he believed in progress and the future of the country. Red tablecloths, carefully ironed, covered the tables, and the chairs, though a bit too sturdy to be fashionable, matched. The same held true for the serviceable white china and the cutlery. Smitty operated a respectable establishment by design. Prostitutes and drifters were not welcome, and gambling was limited to poker games between men of long acquaintance. If you wanted more, the Red River Saloon was just down the street.

The entrance to the dining room was through a pair of withdrawn pocket doors. Josh hesitated between them, his eyes roving about until he spied Doc Cassidy and the town's only lawyer, Pace Granger, seated at a table on the far side of the room. Pace saw him at the same time and waved him over. A thin man with wide, knotty shoulders, Pace specialized in gentle persuasion. Inside and outside a courtroom, he was the calm, collected voice of reason.

A third man present at the table—the rancher, Uriah Thorpe—was tall and barrel-chested. Uriah generally wore a high-peaked Stetson that made him appear even taller. He'd taken it off to reveal a full head of hair that he'd swept back to cover his neck and the collar of his tweed jacket. Beneath the jacket, a watchchain he claimed to be of solid gold crossed a yellow suede vest.

Josh believed that his God commanded him to show charity to all and to love his enemies. He could cite fifty biblical verses, each of them right on point. There was no escaping the mandate, but he had to admit that men like Uriah Thorpe made it hard. In their world, force was king, force of any kind—physical, mental, or financial. Whoever exerted the most force was right by definition.

Josh found the tough talk not only offensive, but craven. Although young enough, Uriah had spent his war years in Cleveland. The Yankee government in Washington had instituted a draft in 1863, a draft you could escape by paying a bounty. That's exactly what Uriah had done. He had paid another man to die in his place.

With no choice, Josh took a seat at Uriah's table. Pace Granger attended services regularly, and Doc Cassidy showed up from time to time. They were neighbors besides.

"We're talkin' about the killing, like everybody else in this town," Doc said as Josh pulled his chair into the table. "Well, you were there, at the house. And I know the sheriff took you out behind the barn where Elijah was attacked."

Doc paused, and Josh knew he was expected to respond, to add his own voice to the gossip. Murder in a community of this size, where everybody knew everybody else, including Elijah Norton, was no small thing.

"I don't know what you want me to say, Doc."

"Well, for starters," Uriah broke in, "we'd like to hear your feelin's on whether or not the beaner done it. Or do you disagree with the sheriff?"

Uriah's tone was close to mocking, his obvious challenge reinforced by a thin smile and a completely artificial Western twang. Josh laid his palms on the table and drew a breath. Patience was called for, but unneeded as it turned out. Pace chose that moment to enter the fray, his tone somehow smooth and sarcastic at the same time.

"Let me fill you in, Reverend. Mr. Thorpe here believes the United States of America—or maybe Texas by itself—should go to war with the sovereign nation of Mexico. That's because Mexican bandits come north a couple of times a year to raid his herd. Never mind that American bandits ride south into Mexico, rustling Mexican cattle, and that both sides have been engagin' in this activity for the past fifty years. Mr. Thorpe has lost a few steers, and a formal declaration of war is therefore mandatory. He's hoping that Francisco will be the match that starts the fire."

Pace was one of the few residents of Whitegrass who didn't depend, at least in part, on Uriah Thorpe. Uriah had come to the region backed by Eastern money, and he used an Eastern law firm with offices in Dallas when he needed assistance. That allowed Pace, who had volunteered for the Confederacy after graduating the College of William and Mary, to speak his mind. Pace had commanded a brigade for Lee at Gettysburg and Richmond. He would not be intimidated by a draft-dodging Yankee.

Doc, by contrast, was temperate by nature. He turned to Josh and asked, "So, tell us what you think, Reverend. You've seen the evidence. You and Schofield were huddled together long enough. Do you think this . . . what's his name?"

"Francisco Rivera," Uriah said. "Mexican cutthroat with no more control of his murderous self than a raidin' Apache."

Doc ignored the rancher's tone. "Yes, Francisco. Do you think he attacked his employer?"

Josh didn't want to take sides, but refusing to answer wasn't an option. He should have known this moment would come when he asked the sheriff what happened. Instead, he'd stumbled into a controversy he would have preferred to avoid. He took a moment to organize his thoughts before he spoke.

"First thing, Francisco claims he's innocent. He hasn't confessed, and he doesn't seem to have a motive, either. So, you have to ask yourself why he stayed at the farm until the sheriff came out instead of making a run for Mexico."

A waiter approached their table at that moment, and Josh ordered the venison stew, the only item on the night's menu that didn't include beef. He paused until the waiter moved off before he spoke again.

"Rachel doesn't believe Francisco to be guilty," Josh said. "She told me so herself. But Francisco was kneeling beside Elijah, his clothes bloody, when Rachel came to find out what happened. And you can see out over the river to at least five miles, but there was no one in sight."

"There, you said it yourself." Uriah leaned over the table. "There was only two people on that farm, and one of 'em attacked Elijah Norton. Lessen you suppose that person to be Rachel, that Mexican did it. But it don't come as no surprise, not to me. Pace says I want a war? Well, the way I see the matter, we already have a war. Face the truth, the Mexicans have to go the way of the Comanche and the Apache. This is a white man's country, and it has been since the first white men landed in Jamestown. One country,

Reverend, from sea to sea. It's our destiny. To stand before it is to stand before the will of the Almighty."

Josh was struck by Uriah's intensity but unsurprised by the sentiment. Uriah had a rival on the range. His full name was Luis Obregon y-Ibarra Diego, but he was universally called Don Diego. With the aid of his vaqueros, Don Diego ran herds that rivaled Uriah's over many thousands of acres on a section of open range he called Rancho Las Cascadas. Once the railroad came through and the range between the Pecos and the Rio Grande opened up, the two men would inevitably go head to head. They were the only ranchers large enough to compete.

About to speak, Josh held his tongue as Paul Wilson stepped into the room. Paul looked about until his eyes found Josh and the others. Then, his face grim, he started over. Josh took that moment, with everyone distracted, to ask a question.

"Does anybody know a cowboy named Cole Bradhurst?"

All three men, including Uriah Thorpe, indicated that they didn't.

Paul reached the table before Josh had time to weigh the consequences of Uriah's denial. "There's trouble," he told the group, "down at the Red River. They're talkin' about lynching Schofield's prisoner."

CHAPTER 11

Cole Bradhurst, even as his boss debated Pace Granger and Josh Hill in the Bright Chance Hotel's dining room, walked into the Red River Saloon. The contrast between the two establishments was startling. Yancey Jackson, the saloon's owner, had invested money in three things only: the roulette wheels, the faro tables, and the silk dresses worn by the women who worked the floor and the cramped bedrooms upstairs. Everything else—floor, ceiling, and walls, tables, chairs, and the long bar—were at best rough-hewn. Given the number of fights that took place, Cole conceded to himself, that was probably the best move on the table. One thing about Yancey, he prided himself on never taking action before he reckoned the odds.

The Red River Saloon was packed when Cole stepped inside, mostly with cowhands from Uriah Thorpe's ranch, the Bar-T, but also with hands from a dozen smaller ranches, maybe forty men in all. This was by design, as was the first move Cole made. He strode to the bar, ignoring the two girls who'd been called to duty, and waved to the bartender, Stewart Greene. Universally called Stoney, the right side of the bartender's face and skull were deeply scarred, the result of a burn. The way Stoney told it, he'd earned the scar fighting a fire in Missouri, his home during the war. But Cole knew that to be untrue. Stoney had been scalded with boiling water by a woman who didn't care for the way he made unwanted advances. That was in Deadwood, South Dakota, where a down-and-out Cole had worked the mines for a long month before deciding that gun-for-hire was infinitely preferable to swinging a pickaxe.

Stoney didn't respond so much to Cole's signal as to the fifty-dollar gold piece he held in his hand. The gold piece also attracted the attention of Yancey. He followed his bartender to where Cole stood, expecting the money to end up in his pocket. He was the boss, after all.

"How do, Cole," Stoney said. As always, the bartender wore a Colt Commander in an elaborate shoulder rig. He also kept a sawed-off twelve-gauge and an oak club originally carved in Ireland behind the bar.

"Doin' just fine, Stoney." Cole nodded to Yancey. "And yourself?"

"Happy as a barkeep in a whorehouse," Stoney replied. "What can I do for ya?"

Cole glanced over his shoulder. "Mr. Thorpe wants to see these boys get to drink their fill tonight." He dropped the gold piece on the bar. "If this don't cover the bill, let me know."

Yancey proved himself quicker than his bartender. He picked up the gold piece and slid it into his pocket. A slender man, Yancey was thought to be quite accomplished with a knife. Tonight, he wore a black silk vest embroidered with a pattern of vines and leaves sewn with gold thread. His bowler hat matched the color of his vest exactly, and his red-leather boots, like Cole's, virtually glowed. Cole watched him walk to the center of the bar, his weight on his toes, his small blue eyes sharp as glass, and reach into the shelf beneath the bar and come up with the club in his hand. He raised the club to shoulder height and slammed it onto the top of the bar. The sudden crash brought everyone to a halt.

"Line 'em up," Yancey instructed his bartender and the two women behind the bar. Then he turned to his patrons. "Let's drink a toast to Elijah Norton," he announced. "On the house."

The cowhands didn't have to be told twice. They bellied up to the bar and took the glasses as fast as Stoney and the two women could fill them. For his part, Cole picked up a glass, then stepped away, satisfied, at least for now, to let events take their course.

Back in Virginia, politicians and their backers used newspapers to sing their praises and attack their enemies, newspapers they usually owned. Whitegrass didn't have a paper, not yet, but every cowhand in Pecos County stopped at the Red River Saloon now and again. Uriah Thorpe wanted the saloon to reflect his own views. More than likely, he'd already spoken to Yancey.

Yancey raised his glass and drank. He waited until the others followed, then laid his glass on the bar. Finally, he spoke. His voice, at first soft and thoughtful, grew increasingly intense.

"Now, I know Elijah Norton wasn't the most popular man out on the range, where y'all make your livin'. He was a dirt farmer, spent his time diggin' and plowin' and frettin' about the weather. Plus, he controlled a section of the river that'd be mighty useful for grazin' the herds you tend. But I'm here to say, and I say it with no apology whatsoever, that Elijah was one of us, a Texan to his bones. His folks come here while most of us were still back East. You think it's dangerous now? You worry about the savages comin' on you when you're far out on that prairie? Well, boys, it was ten times worse for the Norton family, but they never turned tail, never packed their goods and headed back the way they come. They stayed and fought—and as anybody who ever rode past their farm can see for himself, they prospered by their exertions and their pure Texas gumption. Don't forget, them horses you ride are most likely fed on hay that Elijah Norton grew."

Cole finally drained his glass. He'd been ordered to monitor his boss's effort to make the Red River Saloon his in-town headquarters. It was obvious, even now, that he'd succeeded. As for Yancey, it seemed to Cole that the man had anticipated trouble, maybe after talking to Uriah. The Mexican women who often worked at the Red River were nowhere to be found.

"That man, Francisco," Yancey continued, "the man who murdered Elijah Norton? Well, he struck Elijah from behind, smashed his skull right into his brain with a hatchet like a savage. He didn't give Elijah no more chance than Santa Ana did for Will

Travis and Jim Bowie when they stood their ground at the Alamo. No more chance than the Mexican army give to any American soldier taken in battle."

Yancey paused when the cowhands cheered, slapping their hats against their hips, pounding the heels of their boots against the wooden floor. Even forty years later, the Alamo massacre set Texan blood to boiling. Yancey turned to his bartenders and nodded. Once again, the glasses were filled, once again emptied.

Fascinated, Cole gave the exhibition his full attention. The whole business had been organized in haste, and few of the hands were armed. Nothing would happen tonight, not unless the sheriff gave up his prisoner without a fight. But the seeds were being planted, a task that Elijah Norton would have understood only too well. The judge riding circuit in this part of Texas wouldn't pass through Whitegrass for at least three weeks, even longer if he encountered a lengthy trial elsewhere. Uriah Thorpe had all the time in the world, and he'd use it, if Cole was any judge, to build the tension.

"Anyone here remember Goliad?" Yancey asked. "Where that same Santa Ana murdered 450 prisoners? Lined 'em up and had 'em shot dead? And just last year, up to Fort Baxter, Mexican rustlers weren't satisfied with takin' steers. Oh no, they snatched up the cowboys sleepin' in their bedrolls and cut 'em to pieces. Because, y'all must see, that's the way of the Mexican. No regard for human life, no regard whatsoever. And yet this Mexican murderer who goes by the name of Francisco Rivera sits all comfy in his cell, eatin' his dinner while he awaits American justice. Well, Francisco ain't no American, and he never can be, no more than the rest of the Mexicans who infest this land. They got to go, my friends. They got to go back where they come from, if not by choice, then by the actions men like us take. We got to make our intentions clear. This is a white man's country, and won't never belong to no one else."

Yancey signaled once again to his bartender, but this time approached Cole. He spoke directly into Cole's ear, just loud enough to be heard above the general din. "There's torches out behind the building. Uriah asked that I let you know if I got 'em ready in time."

***

Fifteen minutes later, Cole stood in Whitegrass's single street with what had become a mob. Torches threw the normally dark street into moving patterns of light and dark that briefly illuminated the twisted grimaces on the faces of the men as they chanted: "Lynch the Mex, lynch the Mex, lynch the Mex!"

Uriah had shown up by this time, rope in hand, noose already formed. Amused, Cole stood at the edge of the mob, awaiting instructions he knew would never come, at least not tonight. Inside the Red River Saloon, he'd wondered if Sheriff Schofield might not surrender the prisoner without a fight, a gesture that would pretty much assure his reelection for years to come.

That wasn't happening. At the far end of the street, lit by kerosene lanterns hanging from hooks above the doorway, Sheriff Schofield and his deputy sat on wooden chairs. Each man had a double-barrel shotgun lying across his lap. A pair of Winchester repeating rifles, propped against the wall, lay within arm's reach.

Cole didn't know Trey Schofield, had only met him the one time when he had reported the attack on Elijah. That was enough. The man's eyes were flint hard, the eyes of a Texas Ranger, eyes that looked right through you. Not hard enough, though, if he'd arrested Elijah's field hand. Cole's careful preparations, the ranch-hand clothes, the dead deer, the stagecoach for company, and his quiet, respectful manner must have been convincing.

In Cole's judgment, Schofield must surely have been formidable when he was young. That was true of every Texas Ranger he'd ever come across, even if some of them weren't entirely honest. But the sheriff was past his best years, and Cole was confident that if he got within forty feet of Trey Schofield, he could take him out before the shotgun was brought into play.

That wasn't going to happen tonight. Uriah wasn't about to lead a mob of half-drunk, mostly unarmed cowhands into battle. Maybe, Cole thought, it's because he's so tall, because he'd make an easy target. The cattleman, Cole was certain, was as unwilling to risk death from a bullet now than he had been during the war.

"This ain't our night," Uriah told the men, his Texas drawl seeming to Cole especially false. "Go on inside, have another drink, then get yourselves back to whatever ranches you come from. We'll be back tomorrow night—you have my word—and this time we'll be ready."

The men were relieved, despite their howls of protest. Cole read that relief in the tilt of their heads as they poured back into the Red River Saloon. Cowboys reckoned themselves to be tough, but they were a poor match for men like Sheriff Schofield. Maybe armed, with their numbers overwhelming, they'd take a chance. Not under the circumstances, though. They'd settle for their bunks tonight.

"Come with me," Uriah ordered as he started toward the jail.

Uriah, with Cole a pace behind, marched to within ten feet of the sheriff, who didn't so much as twitch at the men's approach. Only when they came to a stop did Schofield speak, and then to Cole, not his boss.

"Evenin', Mr. Bradhurst, it's a real pleasure makin' your acquaintance for a second time."

Cole merely nodded. He wasn't happy to be there, but he'd signed on to be Uriah's personal bodyguard and he had no choice. If Uriah wanted to throw him in the sheriff's face, well—well, he must have his reasons.

"Now, Sheriff," Uriah said, taking a step forward, "I believe you to be a stubborn man. And I didn't have to inquire of your acquaintances to form that judgement. I can see it in your eyes. You ain't never backed down, not once in your whole life, and you're not about to start now. But there's a natural law you might want to consider. Men who don't bend? Sooner or later, they run up against a wind they can't resist. Then they break."

"Is that a threat, Uriah?"

"No, sir. That there is a general observation based on what I've experienced in my own life and the life goin' on around me. Now this here, what happened tonight? It ain't goin' away, and we both know it."

Thus far, Sheriff Schofield hadn't moved a muscle. He sat as relaxed as he would before his own fireplace with his dog at his feet. Nor did his attitude change when he finally spoke, or even when he spit onto the boardwalk an inch from Uriah's lizard-skin boots.

"Why don't you go back out to the ranch, Uriah," he asked, "and shine them fancy boots of yours?"

CHAPTER 12

Josh slept poorly that night, not least because a storm passed only a mile or so from town, close enough for the thunder to vibrate through his bed and the lightning to throw grotesque shadows on the walls of his small bedroom. The storm woke him, but he found it impossible to return to sleep after it passed. What he'd witnessed on the street outside the Red River Saloon troubled him greatly. He'd been through the war, had—he believed—viewed the worst in human nature, seen men become bestial, seen them walk over the bodies of the dead and dying, their eyes unseeing. But war did that—shocked men free of their hearts and souls. War left men cold and empty in the aftermath of battle, left them heartless, left them unfeeling, uncaring.

The hope was that most would recover, that the veterans, once the war ended, would retrieve their hearts. They'd move on to have wives and children and grandchildren, to live productive, meaningful lives. But the screaming, chanting cowboys he'd seen last night—their eyes narrowed, their mouths twisted, their nostrils flared, their skin inflamed—had no excuse. Too young to have fought in the war, they were barely through with being boys, and yet—and yet there they were, screaming for blood.

A passage from Revelation jumped into Josh's mind and wouldn't let go: *And God shall wipe away all tears from their eyes; and there shall be no more death; neither sorrow, nor crying, neither shall there be any more pain: for the former things are passed away.*

How long? How long before men and women were freed from their worst impulses, until the beast in them passed away?

God's children had been waiting for almost two thousand years now, every step forward countered by a step back. The mob, if they'd been able, would have dragged Francisco out of the jail, put a rope around his neck, and let him choke to death. And that's only if they didn't torture him first, if they didn't beat or burn him, all the while rejoicing in his pain.

In only a few hours, Reverend Hill would preside over Elijah Norton's funeral and burial. The situation demanded comfort, a restatement of the most basic Christian beliefs in God's infinite mercy, in the reward due the just, in the fulfillment of the promise that accompanied the birth of Jesus Christ. Any reference to the mundane affairs of men was to be avoided. But the men he'd seen on the street last night weren't all ranch hands. Some were townspeople. Some would be among Elijah's mourners. Some worshipped on the Sabbath at the Whitegrass Community Church.

What, if anything, would he say to them?

To Josh's great relief, even as he set a fire in the cooking stove, Sarah pulled their buckboard to a stop outside the store. He recognized Pharaoh's ornery snort, his outrage. The mule wanted his stall and a bucket of oats.

"You won't believe this," Sarah told her husband as she came through the door.

"Won't believe what?"

"You won't believe who turned up no more than an hour after you left last evening." Sarah didn't wait for her husband to speak. "Carmelita."

A smile pulled slowly at Josh's mouth. "Carmelita Mendoza?"

"The same. She told Rachel that she was raised on a farm and she was here to help. Just walked up to the door and announced her intentions. In addition to general farm work, she told the two of us she'd also cared for her younger brother and sister from when they were babies, so she could help with little Eli if needed."

Josh took Sarah's bag and set it down. Then he embraced and kissed her, as was their habit after even a brief separation. The tradition was a way—or so Josh thought—of renewing their vows.

"What did Rachel say?"

"I believe that Rachel was skeptical at first."

"At first?"

"Well, Carmelita went into the fields to make use of the remaining daylight, while Rachel tended little Eli. I suspect the boy senses that something's happened, something big. I think he can feel the loss coming from his mother. He's always been an easy child, but this time he fussed for an hour before he fell asleep. When he finally did, Rachel put him in a cradle board and we went outside. There was Carmelita, still out in the field, wielding a scythe like it was growing out of her hands. And something more. Carmelita claims she can round up the farmhands Rachel needs to get the crop in."

Still smiling, Josh shook his head. "It appears Carmelita's taken her Christian duties to heart."

"It appears, Josh, that the business about the Lord providing isn't just a heap of empty words. Now let me get breakfast going. Have you finished your eulogy for Elijah's service today or your sermon for church tomorrow?"

"Not yet, but there's something else going on. I don't know if you heard." Josh quickly described the chaos of the night before. He didn't leave Uriah Thorpe out, or Yancey Jackson. Both had stirred up the crowd. Worse yet, the torches they carried hadn't come out of the ground. They'd been prepared in advance. "What I saw last night, it looked spontaneous, but it had to have been organized. And if that's the case, there'll be another attempt tonight, and another tomorrow if tonight's fails."

Josh watched his wife set the kindling afire, then close the oven door. He could hear roosters crowing in the distance. It was barely dawn, and the temperature had dropped into the low seventies, cool enough for a fire and a cooked breakfast. Sarah set a cast iron skillet on the stove, then went to the pantry for flour, baking soda, lard, a plate of dried beef sausages, and a slab of bacon. Biscuits and gravy, all the more comforting for its familiarity on this particular day. The coffee was already bubbling on the stovetop.

"I feel the need to speak out," Josh said. "They plan to lynch Francisco, to hang him without benefit of trial. That's murder."

"If I remember right, we've discussed this in the past."

"And we agreed to let Caesar worry about Caesar's business." Josh walked over to the stove and poured himself a cup of coffee. "We decided to avoid taking sides, but I tell you, Sarah, that the Lord has a way of forcing you to make choices you'd rather not make. Does Rachel still believe Francisco to be innocent?"

"More than ever. And Carmelita too. According to her, Francisco is *el campesino*, a simple farm laborer, tied to the land his entire life. He would be grateful to God for an easygoing employer like Elijah. In many cases, campesinos are worked in gangs, driven hard, and frequently cheated at the end of a harvest."

"But I should still keep my thoughts to myself?"

"I didn't say that. Leave today for a proper mourning. Come tomorrow's Sunday service, you can say whatever your conscience tells you to say. In the meantime, we have a sheriff with years of experience. He can offer the kind of protection your word never will."

Sarah left the stove and walked over to her husband. She laid her hand on his and squeezed gently. "One other thing, Josh, you need to know." She smiled softly. "You're going to become a daddy."

CHAPTER 13

Whitegrass Community Church was full an hour before Elijah Norton's body arrived, with several dozen more gathered outside under the hot sun. Josh was dressed in black, a soldier of Christ in uniform. He wore a collarless white shirt in the traditional fashion, making only one concession to the harsh West Texas summer. The clerical collars he donned during the summer were handmade of soft cotton by Sarah. That was because the stiff collars worn by others chafed Josh's neck hard enough to draw the occasional droplet of blood, especially during the day when his sweat ran freely.

The women among the bystanders carried parasols or wore bonnets, while the men sweated beneath their hats. Fortunately, Uriah Thorpe was not among them.

Josh tried to steer his thoughts from the news Sarah had delivered earlier and focus on the matter at hand. He scrutinized the assembled mourners. Where he recognized one of his congregants, he found room for him or her inside. These were people who knew Elijah and Rachel Norton, while most of the others had never come within a hundred yards of the church. They were ranch hands and farmers, and they were angry, obviously angry—someone had to pay. They muttered as he moved among them, muttered curses loud enough for him to hear.

Josh didn't react, not to their blasphemies or their obscenities. He'd been through war, had witnessed all manner of violent death in the course of his later wanderings. A few words didn't bother him. But he had to wonder about the effect of their outrage on Rachel. Even now, she was probably with Doc Cassidy and Ruddy Robinson, waiting for the lid on Elijah's simple coffin to be nailed down. In a few minutes, she'd leave to bury her husband, the father of her child, and she didn't need this display.

Josh stole a glance at Sarah in her black dress and black veil. They'd been wanting a child for so long that Josh had halfway given up. Now she was two months pregnant, and the urge to protect her and the life she nurtured in her womb rushed over him, as sudden and overwhelming as a flash flood in one of the region's narrow canyons.

And yet, his obligations to God and man remained firmly in place. There was no shirking them, not now, and still be the father he hoped to be.

Josh climbed the steps to the porch that shielded the front of his church from the morning sun. His face stern, his resolve set, he turned to face the crowd. He raised his hands first but did not speak. Instead, he looked past the crowd, out onto the scrubland across the river as a movement caught his eye. Perhaps two hundred yards away, a pair of red wolves alternately dug at what could only have been a burrow. They were too far away for him to make out small details, but one of them suddenly made a snatching motion with his muzzle and both ran away. They were headed, most likely, to their own den with a meal for the pups.

"Gentlemen, ladies," Josh finally said. "Please, give me your attention for just a moment. I'm gonna be brief here and to the point. We're all, including me, outraged by what happened to Elijah Norton. But today, this morning, we've gathered to mourn his passing. Let me say it again: We are here to mourn, and that requires a degree of dignity that I'm expecting all here to demonstrate. Mourning also requires that the deceased's close kin be treated with respect, and I demand that everyone, without exception, show Rachel Norton the respect she deserves. If your outrage has swelled to the point where you don't believe you can demonstrate dignity and show respect, I ask you to leave. Remember, you're standing before God's house. Should you add to Rachel Norton's suffering, you'll be a long while tellin' the Lord how sorry you are."

***

Since Josh had built his church facing the great prairie on the far side of the Pecos River, the only road leading to the church passed through the town, so when Ruddy Robinson's buckboard carrying Elijah's coffin, its sides draped in black bunting, came suddenly into view, it caught all by surprise. The Nortons' buggy, a simple gig pulled by a gray horse, followed closely behind, with Carmelita holding the reins. Rachel sat beside her, head up, chin firm. She held her child in her arms, and her eyes, though focused on some far horizon, were dry.

The crowd became instantly mute, frozen in place, many with their mouths still open as if they'd simply run out of words in midsentence. Only Josh reacted, and even then after a delay. He stepped back into the church and signaled to the pallbearers standing near the door. They came forward, four burly farmers, men who'd known manual labor almost from birth. They took off their hats as they exited the church and approached the make-shift hearse. The other men in the crowd, jolted from their initial paralysis, followed suit, removing their hats and lowering their heads. One of them, a tow-headed cowboy who couldn't have been more than seventeen, stepped up to the buggy and offered the widow his hand.

"Ma'am," he said, helping her down.

Carmelita remained where she was. She wore a gray dress and a matching lace veil. The veil covered her dark hair and left most of her face in deep shadow.

Sarah came out to stand next to Rachel. They didn't embrace but stood side by side, their hands touching. Though the pair faced the church and away from the pallbearers, they couldn't avoid the scraping of Elijah's pine coffin over the bed of Ruddy's buckboard or the slow steps of the pallbearers as they carried the coffin toward the church. Sarah gasped as the coffin passed her, and Rachel tightened the arm that cradled her son. This was final, the last goodbye to what remained of the only man she'd ever loved. The funeral, the burial, then back to a bed he would never again know.

Rachel faltered just a bit as she followed the coffin into the church, as she walked to the front. She stopped by the coffin and laid her palm on top. This far out on the frontier, manufactured coffins of fine hardwood were unknown. Ruddy had crafted the coffin from plain pine boards, then hastily stained it dark brown. The stain was still fresh enough to mark Rachel Norton's hand. She stared at the mark for a moment, as though it was her husband's blood, so recently cleaned from her fingers. Then she bent her head and took her seat.

CHAPTER 14

The Whitegrass Community Church was a simple affair, no more than a room set aside for those times when human beings congregate to affirm their faith in the God who created them. On this day, every bench was filled, and people stood along the walls and at the back. Josh began as he began every service, with the Lord's Prayer. The words he spoke, his voice soft yet firm, came directly from the mouth of Jesus. They were an instruction, and therefore to be taken to heart, especially the most basic entreaty: *Forgive us our trespasses as we forgive those who trespass against us.*

This was, to Josh's mind, one of the central articles of Christian faith. Under other circumstances he would have dwelt on this crucial bargain, this promise made to God by His servants. Not today.

"Elijah Norton," he told the mourners, "was a man of the soil, a man devoted to the cycles of the earth, the growing and the reaping, of course, but the nurturing as well. He knew it wasn't enough to drop seed into the ground, knew he couldn't turn away and wait for his crop to ripen. And so, he toiled through the days and weeks and months, he cultivated his crops, he fulfilled his responsibility as a steward of the earth he tilled. And so, it was, also, with the God that Elijah worshipped.

"I've known some, maybe not a few, who went down to the river, who immersed themselves in the cleansing baptismal waters, but then, as if their work was now done, as if time had stopped, began to coast. Not Elijah Norton. Elijah, as he was a steward of the soil, was a steward of his own soul, a man who put his beliefs into practice. His prayers, as I knew them, were for strength, the strength to practice a simple faith, to hold Jesus always in his heart. Yes, he had his Bible and I know him to have paid close attention to the Gospels, but faith was always central to him. Elijah Norton was a man who could look into his own heart and find his God waiting there."

Josh hesitated for a moment, sensing the wooden cross on the wall behind him, the room's only adornment. What he was going to say next had to be said. But knowing that didn't make it easier.

"Though we never discussed it, I think Elijah knew that he couldn't simply hold the Lord in his heart, that his obligations extended outward, to his fellow travelers, to his community. Nobody who knew Elijah will forget the many kindnesses he showed them, or how quick he was to help in an emergency. And nobody who knew him will ever doubt the love he felt for the woman he called his wife."

Rachel could bear it no longer. The cry that poured from her heart filled the little church. All knew that it surged from the core of her being, that it spoke to unbearable pain. Josh had endured that wail before, and he understood it to carry the sum total of all the suffering—inescapable, inevitable—that humans endure.

Josh found himself wishing that he was more eloquent. Back in Virginia, he'd known ministers who could rattle off a forty-five-minute speech on any topic, even when unprepared. He possessed no such gift, and now, even as his wife took the widow into her arms, he simply waited until the sobs wracking Rachel's body subsided.

"*Jesus wept*," he finally said. "The shortest verse in our Bible, but perhaps the most complex. The story, though, is simple enough. Jesus's cousin and friend, Lazarus, passed away from a sudden, brief illness. When Jesus learned of his cousin's death, He immediately journeyed to the town where Lazarus died. He came upon Mary first, the sister of Lazarus, along with a small crowd of mourners. Mary threw herself at the Master's feet, her suffering so real, so manifest, that Jesus could not avoid the intensity of her grief, or that of the other mourners. The awful pain that tears at human hearts when death claims someone they love was too vivid to be cast aside, and John writes that Jesus was 'deeply troubled' by what He witnessed. So deeply troubled that He literally wept.

"Jesus wept. Even knowing that Lazarus would soon live again, that Lazarus would be resurrected and returned to his family, that the tears they shed, the tears he shared would soon be transformed into laughter and celebration. For Jesus, in raising Lazarus, previewed the gift he would make available to all. Jesus would conquer death, would defy it, would offer the just eternal life, a heaven where families will come together, where husband and wife will be eternally reunited."

Josh looked at Rachel. She sat with her head lowered, seeming lost. He hadn't reached her, but he hadn't expected to. There existed a grief that followed death after a long illness, and a grief that erupted—violent and irresistible—when death is unexpected. Josh went on, nonetheless. He pointed behind him at the simple cross on the back wall. "This was where the promise was kept, on the cross. There Jesus took our pain on himself. There Jesus substituted His own agony for ours. Revelation states the new reality as plainly as it can be stated: *And God shall wipe away all tears from their eyes; and there shall be no more death; neither sorrow, nor crying, neither shall there be any more pain: for the former things are passed away.*"

Josh continued on in that vein for a short time, until he sensed that Rachel could take no more. Then he closed with a short prayer before leading Rachel and Sarah to the front of the church. There he watched the pallbearers, the four simple farmers, take up their burden and carry it, with Rachel following, to the waiting buckboard. Rachel reached out as her husband's remains were lifted into the hearse, her hand rising for a moment before dropping again to her side.

Once the coffin was finally loaded, Rachel climbed into her buggy. She reached back to help Sarah up, then nodded to Carmelita as Ruddy's buckboard, pulled by a black horse, moved off.

The buckboard and buggy covered about a hundred yards before the buckboard pulled to a halt. Elijah was to be buried in the family's cemetery, near his parents and his sister. Those who wished to attend formed up behind Rachel's buggy, a collection of wagons and buckboards and men on horseback.

Josh was first among these, and he slapped the reins against Pharaoh's back as the buckboard and buggy ahead of him moved off, this time more slowly. Elijah's coffin, tied down, was in full view on the buckboard, as were the shoulders and heads of the three women seated in the Nortons' buggy. They sat upright, backs firm, chins up, as was typical of the widows he'd encountered after the war. There had been so many, tied to their children, desperate to survive. He had been staggered by their fortitude, their fundamental bravery as they carried on. They filled the churches on the Sabbath, voices raised, refusing to give up, to cast blame, to demand anything from anybody. It would be no different with Rachel. There would be the gifts, of course, food especially, and perhaps some help with the harvest. But these efforts would fade over time, and Rachel would simply take up the reins of her life, her and her child's, little Eli, who'd begun to cry. Josh watched Rachel settle the infant against her breast. Somehow, women knew how to cope with loss, knew how to bend to the wind, unlike men who tended to break in one way or another. In his mind's eye, Josh saw his own wife bringing their child to her breast. The image, for reasons he could not name, alarmed him.

Far to the west, the clouds began to gather, white becoming gray becoming slate becoming charcoal, finally descending to the prairie below. The lightning strikes came hard and fast, yet the storm was so far away, Josh could hear only a faint rumble, barely as loud as the breeze that flicked past his ears. For a time, the storm appeared to move in unison with the funeral procession, its shadow dancing across the scrubland until the Norton farm came into view. Only then did it finally dissipate. Only then did the sky above clear. The grave was already dug, with ropes set on the ground to lower the coffin. At the head of the grave, a pair of spades topped a dirt mound, perhaps the same spades used in Elijah's gardens, spades that had known his callused hands.

Josh kept his final words simple. He spoke again of Elijah—gentle, faithful, a man of obligations freely chosen and met, taken from us far too soon. Rachel stood by the coffin, not weeping, not yet, only exhausted, as if the last bit of energy had been drawn from her body. Josh realized the woman had reached her limit and he quickly finished with a quote from 1 Thessalonians: *I do not want you to be ignorant, brethren, concerning those who have fallen asleep, lest you sorrow, like others who have no hope. For if we believe that Jesus died and rose again, even so God will bring with Jesus those who have fallen asleep in him.*

Josh stepped away from the open grave, as did Rachel and Sarah. He nodded to the pallbearers and they picked up the ropes stretched beneath the coffin, prepared to lower it into the earth. But Rachel could contain herself no longer. She fell on the coffin and sobbed, her broken heart all but visible to the men and women who bore witness. Josh fought his own tears. God had given a great gift to His people, the gift of love, but it came with a price. He knew the pain that tore at his own heart was nothing compared to what Rachel suffered. It hurt nonetheless, hurt him bad, and it didn't vanish when Rachel called her husband's name, as though she expected him at any moment to appear by her side, smiling that ready smile she knew so well.

"Elijah, Elijah, Elijah, Elijah, oh my darling Elijah."

CHAPTER 15

There was food to be had after the burial, and Josh, though far from hungry, nibbled at the offerings for an hour. He took that time to ask as many of the other mourners as possible if they knew a cowhand named Cole Bradhurst. Harry Nance, one of the few ranchers friendly to Elijah and a regular churchgoer, was the only man to respond positively.

"Met the man once," he told Josh, "but I ain't known him to be a cowhand. Dressed like a dude when I come across him in the company of Uriah Thorpe. Took him to be Uriah's personal bodyguard."

Josh didn't belabor the point, didn't ask for details. Sarah was staying overnight with Rachel at the Norton farm, and she'd need the buckboard in the morning. When he was offered a ride into Whitegrass by the town's cooper, Abe Jordan, and his wife, Clementine, a buxom woman universally called Clemmie, he took it.

A mute from birth, though he heard perfectly well, Abe communicated with his wife, Clemmie, in sign language, trusting her to relay any messages. The arrangement suited Clemmie, who knew everybody in town and a few of the families out on the prairie. In local political matters, the matters Josh tried so hard to avoid, she was a force to be reckoned with.

On this day, her powdered face streaked with tears, Clemmie was unusually quiet as they made their way along the trail. When the church came into view, she spoke her mind.

"This is tearin' me up, Reverend," she said. "I'm proud to claim Elijah and Rachel as my true friends, and puttin' Elijah in the earth has surely taken its toll on my spirits. But this business in town, it needs addressin'."

"You're talking about what happened last night." It wasn't a question, the way Josh put it.

"We're bein' stampeded by Uriah Thorpe and his like." Clemmie's own alliances were known to all. Abe sold most of his barrels and crates to the local farmers at harvest time, and she supported their right to a fair portion of the open lands west of the Pecos. But Clemmie, prejudiced or not, had made a valid point, and Josh couldn't deny it. Uriah hoped to achieve his goals, whatever they were, before an opposition could be organized. "I don't like it, Reverend, and folks need to speak out."

Tomorrow was the Sabbath, and Josh would deliver a sermon, as he did every Sunday. The Jordans would be there, and Clemmie's message was plain enough. The "folks" she spoke of included Reverend Josh Hill.

Abe chose that moment to fire off a barrage of hand signs. Clemmie nodded as he went along, turning to Josh only when Abe settled down.

"The farmers will be next," Clemmie said. "That's Abe's point. The Mexican ranchers first, then the farmers. We won't be needed for produce no more, Reverend, not once the railroad comes through. We'll get oranges out of California all year round."

Certain matters were left unsaid, but only because they were familiar to Josh. The soil out on the scrubland between the Pecos and the Rio Grande was fertile enough to grow crops, including oranges, if you could get water to it. Rainfall was too scant and too unreliable to fill that role. But there were natural springs throughout the area. The Indians knew them all, but ranchers, too, relied on springs to water their herds. Farmers contended that the springs resulted from water contained in an aquifer being forced to the surface, water that could be reached by the drilling techniques used in the California citrus groves. If they were right, farming could easily compete with ranching as the area's dominant industry. Yet most of the farmers, along with Clemmie, believed that the ranchers, led by Uriah, would never let that happen.

White farmers, white ranchers, Mexican farmers, Mexican ranchers, town interests, range interests. To Josh, it seemed there were as many sides as there were ambitions, with West Texas a bag of prizes there for the grabbing.

Josh rode past the church to his store, where he thanked the Jordans for the ride, then set up shop. To his surprise, Whitegrass Mercantile grew busy, though more came to gossip than to buy. A mix of farmers and cowboys, they broke about even between those who wanted to hang Francisco then and there, and those who demanded that the law prevail, like it or not. But even these latter, it seemed obvious to Josh, had already convicted Francisco. Their position was simple enough. If the end result is the same, why not wait? Why not observe the formalities? Why not show the rest of the country, and especially the Southern-Pacific railroad, that Whitegrass does not lie outside the boundaries of civilization? Why not show the railroad that Whitegrass was ready to be integrated into the nation's economy?

Josh absorbed the opinions as they came at him, until Judah Burke pushed through the doors. He'd been to the morning funeral service but had not attended the burial.

"You forgot your shadow," Josh said, his tone light enough to be teasing.

"You mean Paul?" Judah wore a sable-brushed cotton jacket with tails that hung below the seat of his matching trousers. In no hurry, he withdrew a white handkerchief from the jacket's inside pocket and wiped his face. "Left him at the store. Ranchers are stockin' up, Reverend. Feel there's somethin' big comin' and they don't wanna see their animals go unfed."

Josh busied himself for a moment with a pile of tobacco plugs he'd been sorting, then said, "And what would that something be?"

"Can't say." Judah cleared his throat. "Saw that Mexican gal with Rachel this morning."

"Judah, I believe that you and I have already covered this ground."

"Right you are, Reverend. Everything we have to say on the subject has already been said. But I haven't come to talk about that woman. She's not your burden, not no longer. She's Rachel's now. No, I come because respectable folks in this town listen to you. Francisco? Face it, Reverend, he's as good as gone, one way or t'other. Personally, I say get it done tonight. Get it done and get back to work, the town up and running. But I'm not stupid. I know there's others that think different, and I'm here to find out if you're one of 'em."

"Under our constitutions, federal and Texan, Francisco's entitled to a trial. I believe in the law, Judah, and not in chaos."

"Well, maybe you should start takin' your guidance from the Bible. An eye for an eye, Reverend. That's the way my Bible reads."

Josh might have argued the point but chose not to prolong the confrontation. His voice betrayed his irritation when he finally replied, despite his best efforts. "Anything else I can do for you?" he asked.

"Yes, there is. You can take a piece of advice. All the time you been in Whitegrass, you and the missus, you stayed clear of town affairs. You might have been our conscience in a general sense, but you never took sides on a particular dispute. Be a real good idea to keep it that way, Reverend. There's men of . . . of influence? Yes, men of influence who won't forget, maybe when the town grows and you find yourself with competitors."

Twenty minutes later, Sheriff Schofield, bearing a shotgun, walked into the store. He seemed tired to Josh, tired and under a great strain, an elected official forced to thwart the will of the citizens who voted for him. Not all, by any means, but enough to pretty much guarantee he'd be unemployed come November's election.

"I s'pose you saw what happened last night," Schofield told Josh after an exchange of pleasantries.

"Yes sir, I did."

The sheriff pointed to a box of nickel cigars. "Take five of those, Reverend, and a box of matches."

"Thought you gave 'em up, Trey."

"Thought I did too, but these are some ugly times." He took one of the cigars and put it in his mouth but didn't light it. "This is stupidity. Hear me? Sheer stupidity. Folks in this town pay me to keep order, to enforce a set of laws they made for themselves. They need that order, ya see, so they can go about the business of makin' money. Now they're prepared to throw those laws out the window, or at least the one that entitles a man to a fair trial by a jury of his peers."

"Not everyone." Josh described his conversation with Abe and Clemmie.

Trey snorted. "You think Abe and Clemmie'll show up tonight, maybe put themselves between Francisco and the mob?"

"That what you need?"

"No, what I need is you, Josh. I'm lookin' for volunteers I can deputize under the authority given to me by the town council. I'd like to count you among them. You and I been huntin' more than once, and I know you to be a dead shot. And you were a lawman too, so you know when to shoot and when to hold fire. Reverend, this town's near to explodin' . . ."

Josh cut him off. "What about Francisco? What's the point of protecting him if you don't investigate the murder? Rachel doesn't think he's guilty, and neither do I. It just doesn't make sense, him sticking around until you showed up. And that cowboy who notified you, Cole Bradhurst? He's not a cowboy, Sheriff. From what I hear, the man's a hired gun."

The statement caught Sheriff Schofield off guard. He looked down at the floor, his eyes fixed on the tips of his boots. "Will say this," he finally muttered, "it don't hardly matter who hit Elijah with that hatchet iffen I don't keep Francisco alive. But I will make you this promise. If matters calm somewhat, I will do my job. I will investigate." Schofield finally lit his cigar, bringing the match up along his thigh. He puffed for a moment, then drew in a lungful of smoke, his eyes closing as he exhaled. "Now, about you deputizin' up, Reverend," he finally said. "I need a yes or a no."

Josh shook his head, the gesture firm, despite a faint sense that he could not, with Sarah pregnant, risk his own life if he meant to protect her. His motives were far from unmixed. "I know you got to do whatever's necessary to protect your prisoner," he finally said. "But my killing days have been over for some time, my fighting days, too. I serve a different Master now."

CHAPTER 16

To Cole Bradhurst, Saturday night's revels at the Red River Saloon were no more than a reenactment of the previous night's—with one exception. There were a lot more guns in evidence this time. Long guns, mostly—Sharps, Henrys, shotguns, and a few Winchesters—all stacked by the door. The guns had been waiting for the cowboys when they wandered into the saloon after a day at work. Cole didn't ask the bartender, Stoney, where the ordnance had come from. One way or another, he knew, it flowed from Uriah, his boss.

Well, Cole thought as he stood off to the side, his arm around a young woman named Grace, it's easy to put a gun in a cowboy's hand. Anyone can pull a trigger, but killing a man is a different matter when bullets are coming back at you, especially if you're too young to have known war. No, he concluded, these boys will have to be led—stampeded, really—into battle. That would be his job.

Cole slapped Grace on her backside. "Be off, girl. There's work to be done."

Short and pretty, Grace flashed her favorite pout, which she assumed to be irresistible. "This business with that Mexican . . . well, it's ruinin' *my* business, Cole. Promise you'll finish it tonight and come back to your sweetheart."

"Can't promise the former, Grace, but if I'm still breathin', you can pretty much count on the latter."

Cole threw Grace a wink as he walked over to the bar. There he joined two men who were drinking steadily, a bad sign in his opinion. The shorter of the two was a barrel-chested frontiers-

PREACHER OF THE PECOS

man named George Thompson. The bearded George claimed to
have guided a hundred wagon trains across the plains at a time
when buffalo herds numbered in the millions and the Sioux ran
wild across the Dakotas. The completion of the Union-Pacific
had marked the end of that era, after which George had turned
renegade, selling his skills to the highest bidder.

The second man, younger and taller, went by the name of
Irish Jack Kelly. He claimed to have run with Bloody Bill Ander-
son during the war, and with the James gang afterward. Cole had
no opinion as to the man's truthfulness, one way or the other. It
seemed like every man on the frontier fought in the war, the only
difference being for which side. But Irish Jack's brogue was real
enough, and Cole was pretty sure the man would be dead game
in a fight. Whether he'd also remain calm, however, whether he'd
take orders, was a question still to be answered.

"Ah, boss, don't see why we're about wastin' time." Irish
Jack's brogue was thick enough to cut. "Let's just get it done, the
three of us."

Cole ignored the suggestion. Instead, he told both men, "I'd
appreciate you stoppin' your drinkin'. And I do mean now."
Cole's specialty, carefully cultivated, was a steely calm designed
to make other men uneasy. He projected that calm and confidence
now. Don't even think, his eyes told both men, about challenging
my authority. "Bad enough I have to deal with these drunk cowhands. I need you men sober enough to take orders."

Irish Jack, for his part, was glad, although he didn't show it.
New to town, he was unfamiliar with the dynamics of the situation and smart enough to admit the fact, at least to himself.
George, on the other hand, still appeared defiant to Cole. Most
likely, the man had come out of the womb with a bottle in his
hand. But he didn't argue the point, and Cole let the matter drop
as Yancey banged the top of the bar.

"Went to a funeral today." Yancey nodded to Stoney, then
waited until every spectator held a glass in his hand before he
repeated himself.

"Went to a funeral today. Saw me a woman there holdin' a babe in her arms, tears pourin' down. Because, you see, that body in the coffin just a few feet from where she stood belonged to her husband. His name was Elijah Norton, and he never done harm to no man, not in his entire life. No, Elijah was a man who tended his family the way he tended his fields, with great care, with tenderness, with love."

Cole smiled to himself. Yancey had stolen the sentiment from Reverend Hill's eulogy. Now he was using Hill's words to produce a result the reverend never intended.

"Elijah's passin' would be a tragedy, sure enough, even if his death had been caused by one of the many illnesses that plague our times. Smallpox, maybe, or dysentery or cholera or yellow fever or consumption." Yancey paused, his eyes swinging across the audience, back and forth, taking his time. When he finally spoke again, his tone was sharper, his voice louder.

"But that ain't what happened to Elijah. He wasn't struck down by some disease that couldn't be seen comin'. It was another human bein' that brought on Rachel Norton's tears. It was a man, a cold-blooded murderer who broke her heart, who made that babe she held in her arms a near orphan. That man's name is Francisco Rivera, a man given work by Elijah Norton, a man Elijah trusted, a man who thanked Elijah by taking up a hatchet and smashing it into his benefactor's skull."

Yancey slammed the club onto the top of the bar. "One blow delivered with force enough to drive the man's skull into his brain, to deliver an injury from which no man recovers. Now imagine Rachel, this most loving of wives, standing by while the only man she'd ever touched slowly expired, while his life drifted away. Rachel watched Elijah draw his last breath, watched his chest rise and fall one final time. She closed his eyes, cleansed his cooling flesh, all the time with a babe in arms and a crop in the field, wonderin' how she was gonna survive. And here's the worst, boys, that coward sittin' in Sheriff Schofield's jail stood right beside her, pretendin' to help, pretendin' to care. But ain't that the way? Ain't that the way of the Mexican thief, the assassin in the night? Why, in all my days, I never seen a Mex stand up to a fair fight. No, when you and a Mex stand face-to-face, it's all, *Sí, señor.* But don't turn your backs, men, 'cause iffen ya do, you'll find a knife drove deep into it."

Cole had to admit it. Yancey had the gift. The cowhands in the room, many of whom had attended the funeral, hung on every word the man spoke. Cole had also been to the funeral but had remained outside the church, on the edge of the crowd. He hadn't been wearing the double-breasted Cavendish vest he wore now, or the sharply creased black trousers, or the flat-crowned plantation hat, or the Colt in its hand-tooled holster. No, he'd appeared as an ordinary cowhand and stayed long enough to see the truth of Rachel's suffering for himself. Knowing all the while that he'd been the cause.

Well, he told himself as Yancey went on, the man could've saved himself. Elijah could have sold the farm and walked away a man of means. He could have . . .

"All right, boys," Yancey shouted. "What do you say? Are you gonna let that Mex sit in his cell, chewin' on his sweet potatoes, settlin' in for a good night's rest? Or are you gonna stand up and be men?"

Cole, Irish Jack, and George were ready when Yancey led the mob out of the saloon. Each man, as he passed, was handed a loaded rifle and a handful of cartridges. Maybe they'd know how to use them, maybe not. Enraged and determined, they didn't seem to care, which made them, in Cole's opinion, utter fools. He'd counted too many bodies to risk his own life for any principle, worthy or unworthy. Money, on the other hand . . .

Uriah awaited them in the street. He'd already lit one torch and had a dozen others at the ready. The torches were taken up and lit within seconds.

"Keep in mind, men," Uriah shouted. "God Almighty set this country aside for white men. He means for us to rule this land from one sea to another. But He won't do it for us, boys. No, sir. The Lord has demanded that we prove ourselves worthy by doin' it for ourselves. Well, we've done what He asked. We've enacted His will across most of this here land, from Massachusetts to California. Let's do it for West Texas. Right this minute, boys. Let's make West Texas a white man's country." The rancher paused long enough to hold up a noose. "No backward steps now. Let's get it done."

Cole kept to the side as the mob advanced. Although he was on full alert, eyes raking the windows and rooftops he passed, he found himself unprepared when the preacher stepped out into the street, placing himself between the mob and the jail. It took Cole a moment to remember the man's name, but then it came back to him: Reverend Josh Hill, who owned the general store. The preacher was unarmed, but he stood tall, his back straight, apparently unafraid. And apparently stupid. Cole couldn't hear what the man was shouting over the shouting of the mob, but whatever it was, it didn't hinder the advance. The preacher was pushed back first, then brushed to the side. He fell as Cole came abreast, not attacked, but dismissed.

Uriah brought the crowd to a halt just past the cistern. The sheriff and his deputy had risen as the mob approached. They stood now, double-barreled shotguns at the ready, Winchesters behind them. Cole recognized the tactic. They would fire four rounds of buckshot into the crowd, hoping to induce panic, then grab the Winchesters and retreat into the jail. It wouldn't work, but it was all they had. Cole was certain that between Irish Jack and himself, the sheriff and his deputy could be eliminated. In fact, given the first move, he was pretty sure he could do the job on his own. True, the shotguns would likely be fired and there'd be casualties, with maybe Cole among them, but at the end of the fight, the jail would be unprotected.

"Sheriff Schofield," Uriah shouted. "We come for that Mex killer you got all nice and cozy in a cell. We mean to have him."

"Not tonight, Uriah."

"That right? I notice you skipped Elijah's funeral. That because you're more interested in protectin' a killer than payin' your respects to a grievin' widow?"

Cole watched his boss closely, looking for a signal they'd arranged at the ranch. If Uriah wanted an attack launched, he'd take out a blue handkerchief and wipe his face. Just now, the mob he led was as restless as it was outraged. That some eager, half-drunk cowboy would fire off a shot and trigger an all-out battle, which would become more and more likely as time went on. But then Sheriff Schofield pulled back the hammers on the shotgun, the clicks somehow louder than the shouted threats of the cowhands, and the fight was essentially over.

Five men concealed on the roof of the jail rose to one knee, their Winchesters at the ready. The quiet they inspired was profound enough for Cole to hear the hoot of a barn owl perched on the stable's weather vane that sometimes served as a lightning rod. Cole recognized only one of the five—the lawyer, Pace Granger—but all appeared ready to put up a fight, even though badly outnumbered.

Cole took stock of the situation. The cistern with its stone parapet was only a short distance behind them. A well-organized company would retreat to the cistern, firing as they went, and take cover behind it. That wasn't going to happen. It wasn't going to happen because both shotguns and at least two of the rifles were pointing at Uriah's chest.

After a moment, Cole caught the attention of Irish Jack and George. He signaled them by raising his hand, palm down, and swiping it from left to right. Both men nodded. It wasn't happening, not tonight. No, tonight they'd return to the Red River Saloon and whatever pleasures awaited them.

"Sheriff Schofield," Uriah declared, "I think you're a dang fool. But if you want an all-out war, you'll have one."

"Lookin' forward to it, Uriah. Ain't had me a real war since I left the Rangers. Now, you take these poor fools and be off. It's past my supper time, and I get right grouchy when my stomach rumbles."

"Are you tellin' me what to do now, Schofield?"

"What I'm tellin you, Mr. Thorpe, is that if any man among you raises his weapon, I will send you off to count cows in hell."

CHAPTER 17

Reverend Hill's sleep was filled with images that fought each other, fang and claw, as if for possession of his very soul. Rachel Norton appeared over and over again—little Eli cradled in her arms, held close to her bosom—her expression at once stricken and fiercely protective. Sarah too appeared, not as she was, but as she would be months from now, her womb full, her arms cradled beneath her swollen belly as if she already held her unborn child. Sarah's blue eyes stared straight ahead, stared into his, the eyes he'd come to love filled with hope for the future. He'd wanted, in his dreams, to go to her, to gently hold her in his arms, to place a gentle kiss on her lips. He imagined her laughing at him, at the care he took, as if she was some fragile vase that might, at any moment, shatter.

In Josh's dream, he never got to hold his wife, because even as he took a step, her image was replaced by an oncoming mob. Josh had stood his ground as they approached, lecturing them on justice, though he knew, even while they milled about in front of the Red River, that they would not understand, would not even hear a word he said. He was tempted to define their collective expression with words like bestial, inhuman, foul, and cruel, but there was something else there, a quality he was reluctant to admit but could not escape. They projected righteousness from every pore, and Josh had known, even as he was brushed aside, that these men, each of them, believed he was doing God's work.

The God that Josh and Sarah Hill worshipped did not demand hate. That was the first thought to touch Josh's mind when he awakened in the middle of the night. Only it wasn't true, and he'd read his Bible thoroughly enough to know it. God himself, the God of the Hebrews, could hate, as Proverbs noted: *There are six things the Lord hates, seven that are an abomination to him.*

There existed plenty of room for human hate as well, a passage from Ecclesiastes, familiar enough to be known by every Christian, left no room for doubt: *A time to love and a time to hate; a time for war, and a time for peace.*

Josh slept again, fitfully, as before, drawn to Rachel and her child, and to Sarah's beautiful, knowing smile. He saw the mob again, but this time he seemed prepared. How many times in human history had mobs gathered to wreak havoc on the guilty or the innocent? Yes, opposition was appropriate, even obligatory, but not surprise or shock.

***

At daybreak, Josh stood on the porch of his church. Though still below the horizon, the sun's first rays found a thin line of clouds, tinting their edges crimson, the new light dispersing the lazy shadows from the prairie. Yet even as this display moved him profoundly, Josh found himself wishing that Sarah was here to advise him, wishing it was Monday and not the Sabbath, wishing that the growing burden could be somehow lifted. But it was indeed the Sabbath, there was no escaping the fact, and Sarah, as she comforted her grieving friend, pursued an obligation far more profound than offering advice to her husband. He was on his own for the moment, his choices his own to make.

Josh wasn't hurt or offended by what had transpired on the prior night. The mob's reaction to him had been anything but personal. He doubted that most of them even knew who he was. To them, he was a temporary fence, an obstacle, and not a very large one at that. So, no, standing in the middle of the road with one hand in the air wasn't going to do it. Nevertheless, he'd taken a stand when he marched into the street, driven by an impulse he couldn't resist, a reality that carried implications he was only beginning to comprehend.

For a long moment, Josh watched the sun's rays cut between the clouds, filling every gap, finding their way to a higher layer of flat cloud. He might have remained there for a longer time, lost in the moment, but his small reverie was interrupted by the appearance of the lawyer, Pace Granger.

"Never did sleep well," Pace said, his smile apologetic. "Early morning's the worst, so I take walks. Don't want to disturb Mary Ellen. No, no, Reverend, now there's a woman who sleeps hard and wakes up mean. Funny part about it, an hour later, after she's had her breakfast, she becomes an angel."

Josh shook the lawyer's hand. Were they allies now? Had he, Josh, taken sides, one neighbor against another?

"Your walks take you to the church often, Pace?"

"As a matter of fact, the way you set the church up, with its back to the town and the view out over the prairie, the porch here is the most peaceful place I know. But it's just as well I ran into you." Pace tucked his thumbs behind his lapels. "I've become Francisco Rivera's lawyer, officially. As befits my role, I spoke to Francisco first thing, and Sheriff Schofield right after. Now my talk with Francisco didn't come to more than him denying the crime. But the sheriff was straightforward. Francisco's guilty, according to Schofield, because there was no one else to commit the crime. Francisco's motives don't matter. Him not running off to Mexico doesn't matter, either. Francisco murdered Elijah Norton because Francisco was the only one at the farm, except Rachel with little Eli."

Josh smiled as he found himself responding to Pace's smooth, even tones. The words slipped from the lawyer's mouth like honey poured from a jar, only to bite when you swallowed them down.

"Doesn't seem like a whole lot of evidence," Josh said.

"It will to a jury that's already convicted my client, which is the jury he'd get if the trial was held today." Pace took a cigar from his pocket, one of the five-cent specials from Whitegrass Mercantile, and lit up. "My strategy, the only one I've got, is to prove that someone other than Francisco might have committed this crime. I don't have to name that person. If it could have been someone else, then Francisco's not running off looms large. Rachel's opinion, too. According to Rachel, Francisco was a passive man, mild as milk, interested only in sending money home to his family. That's where the lack of motive comes in . . ."

Pace shrugged as he lapsed into silence, his smile widening. After a moment, he straightened his bony shoulders and groaned. "Swear, Reverend, the aches and pains just keep coming these days."

Josh nodded. Pace had something on his mind other than the sunrise or not disturbing Mary Ellen's sleep. "Sounds like you have things under control," he said.

"Wish that was true. But there's still the part about convincing a jury someone else might have committed the crime. I haven't started investigating, but I think I can pull that off. It's the other part that mostly troubles me, the part about jurors who've already made up their minds. It's been my personal experience, all through my life, that men don't readily admit to being in error. Once they set their minds on a belief, they're hard put to make a change."

The temperature, this early in the morning, was still in the low seventies, the dry air invigorating. Yet Josh was aware of neither as he tugged at a loose bit of yarn in the well-patched sweater he wore. "You mind getting to the point, Pace?" he finally asked. "Bein' as I have a sermon to get ready for."

"Fair enough, Reverend. The point here is that, if we're gonna change minds, we need to start now. There are men and women in this town who believe in the rule of law. Right now, they're just keeping to themselves while they gauge the flow of events. They're not exactly afraid, but they have no desire to run afoul of men like Uriah Thorpe for a lost cause. Someone needs to step up, to bring them together."

"And that would be me, Pace? This morning when I deliver my sermon?"

"You've read my mind. People look up to you, Reverend. I believe more than you realize. What you say matters." Pace hesitated for a moment, before concluding. "And what you don't say, if you play it safe, will also matter."

CHAPTER 18

Whitegrass Community Church, as Josh stood by the door greeting his congregation, was already crowded at ten o'clock. Almost every merchant in town, families in tow, had already made an appearance, and the little church was full up. This was Pace's work, or so Josh concluded. He'd brought the families around Whitegrass with the most to lose from a breakdown in law and order to Josh's church. Josh had never known the lawyer to be a gambler, but he was taking a chance now. Earlier, Josh had offered no guarantees.

Josh was about to turn toward the pulpit when Rachel Norton's buggy rounded the corner and pulled up outside the church. Carmelita held the reins, her touch sure, with Sarah and Rachel, her sleeping child in a sling, sitting to her right. Josh nodded to himself. He should have expected this. Rachel's features were drawn, but her blue eyes hinted at a determination that seemed almost ferocious.

Sarah paused long enough to kiss her husband on the cheek before entering the church but said nothing. Rachel and Carmelita passed with barely a nod. Josh waited until the others made room for them to sit, then walked to the pulpit, hoping his step was firm despite an inner turmoil that would not be resolved. He surveyed his congregation for a moment, noting the presence of Uriah Thorpe. Uriah was accompanied by a tall man in his forties. The man's expression, bolstered by his sandy hair and a spray of freckles over the bridge of his nose, seemed innocent and eager, as if he couldn't wait to find out what would happen next. Josh wasn't fooled. He was looking at Cole Bradhurst, and he knew it.

"Let us pray," Josh said, pleased to find his voice firm. "Let us pray for the farmers' harvests. Let us pray for the great herds on the prairie. Let us pray that the hailstorms sure to come do harm to neither. For the Lord in His wisdom chose to make this world complex instead of simple. He chose to place all creatures great and small on our earth, chose to separate land and water, to leave the stars in the sky and the rocks in the ground. Of course, we know that each of these things I've named, and a myriad more, rise and fall at His command. And yet all appears mysterious to creatures as insignificant as ourselves, the whys and the wherefores obscure, until at times, in our ignorance, we grow fearful.

"And so, in our humility, we pray. We pray for guidance, a path through the darkness, and we thank the good Lord with all our hearts. For the God we worship, the God you've come here to serve on His day, has placed His guidance in plain sight." Josh raised his Bible, turning to the left, then to the right. "The Word of the Lord, my friends, the Word embraced by every Christian, because you cannot be a Christian and reject the Bible. You cannot."

Josh stepped away from the pulpit. Again, he surveyed his congregation. They didn't know where he was going, but he definitely had their attention.

"John tells us a story about Jesus," Josh began, "and a woman accused of adultery. Jesus is in Jerusalem and He rises early on this particular morning. He rises early and walks from the Mount of Olives to the great temple where, according to John, He '*sat down and began to teach.*' His followers must have been there waiting for him, along with the curious and perhaps a disciple or two, because one senses, reading the verses, that this was business as usual. Jesus is referred to as Master or Teacher, even by the Pharisees.

"But if the morning began as an ordinary morning in Jerusalem, it didn't remain ordinary for long. It was still early when a mob suddenly appeared, led by Pharisees and scribes, a mob dragging a woman along with them, a mob who '*set her in the midst.*' The woman, Jesus was told, had been caught red-handed in the arms of a man not her husband. The penalty under Mosaic law was death, as the Pharisees claimed, but not this way, not dragged off by a raging mob, not stoned to death without trial, without any chance to defend herself. And make no mistake, the Hebrews of that time had courts, called *beit din*, along with a well-developed body of laws, called *halakhah*. This woman could have been accused, could have been tried. But the mob that threw her to the ground in front of Jesus and His followers meant to dispense its own justice, then and there. Would Jesus object? After all, Mosaic law does call for adulterers to be executed.

"Of course, we all know that Jesus was a step ahead of the mob. He didn't argue the law. He shamed them by demanding that only '*He who is without sin cast the first stone.*' No one in the mob, not the most ardent Pharisee, was prepared to make that claim, no more than anyone in this room would dare to claim perfect innocence. This is why we let justice take its course, this frank admission of our own imperfections. For the Pharisees' claim, that in stoning this woman, they would merely be following the law of Moses, is utterly false. Mosaic law calls for trials to determine guilt and makes specific rules about witnesses and evidence to be considered, just as the laws of Texas and the United States demand that a man accused of a crime—even the crime of murder, even if he's Mexican—be given a chance to defend himself before a jury of his peers."

Josh stopped there, his eyes darting from face to face, almost daring any of his congregants to dispute this claim. No one did, not even Uriah, whose face and neck had grown red. The owners of virtually every business in Whitegrass were seated around him. They were not violent men, though most had fought in the war, but they controlled the town's politics. They were men and women of influence.

"I'm going to tell you one more story. From Exodus 18." Josh's gaze settled for a moment on his wife, Sarah. Her smile was small, small enough to be mistaken for the normal set of her mouth by any but the man who'd taken her to wed. Sarah approved. She was on his side, maybe even proud of him. "This story is about fatherly advice, specifically the advice given to Moses by Jethro, his father-in-law. The Children of God, the Hebrew people, are still in the wilderness when Jethro comes to visit. Now, Jethro's a respected priest in his own right, and Exodus tells us that Moses bowed before him." Josh smiled, and his tone became more intimate. "Well, folks, a visit from a man as wise and influential as Jethro would have been cause enough for celebration, but Jethro, Moses's father-in-law, brought Moses's wife, Zipporah, and their two children with him, so the occasion was truly joyous. In fact, Moses tells us that Aaron and all the elders of Israel feasted with Jethro that evening. Now, you'd think, reading this part of the chapter, that Jethro's visit would be the whole point. But it isn't, my friends. Jethro's got a more important role to play." Josh repeated himself. "Far more important.

"Next day, Jethro was more or less wandering through the camp—a camp that included, by the way, all of the Israelites—when he came upon Moses sitting in judgment, a special job that had fallen to him. There were so many petitioners, it's written, that the people had to stand before him all day, voicing their disputes, one after another after another. Naturally, Jethro was appalled by what he saw. Surely, the spiritual and political leader of the Israelites has better things to do than settle a dispute over two cows and a chicken." Josh paused, allowing his congregation to enjoy their small smiles. "That evening, when Jethro asked Moses for an explanation, Moses told him, '*The people come to me and ask me to ask for God's decision about their problems. If people have an argument, they come to me, and I decide which person is right. In this way, I teach the people about God's laws and teachings.*' Well, Jethro couldn't believe what he was hearing and took Moses to task, mincing no words. '*This isn't the right way to do this.*'

"Jethro's advice was direct and to the point. His instructions were equally direct. *'Choose good men you can trust—men who respect God. Choose men who will not change their decision over money. Make these men judges of the people. There should be judges over one thousand people, one hundred people, fifty people, and even over ten people. Let these judges judge the people.'*" Josh laid the Bible on the pulpit and folded his hands. "Let's take a step back. Let's take a longer view. The Israelites, going back generations, have been slaves in Egypt, and slaves don't get to judge themselves. Slaves are judged by their masters. But the Hebrews are now free, led from bondage by Moses, and they must resolve their own disputes. Will they fall into chaos? Into anarchy? Every man for himself? That was never a possibility, not if they were to survive as a people. No, a system was needed, a system of justice the Hebrew people could rely on, and Jethro helped create it. Although Jethro left for home a short time later, Exodus tells us that Moses took his advice, creating the judges needed to keep order."

Josh took a deep breath. The point of his sermon wasn't all that subtle, and he was sure his listeners got it. How they'd take it, though, was anyone's guess.

"Let me just finish with this. I spent most of last night with the Good Book. I had my Bible study books out, too. I was looking for one instance, just one, where the God we love and worship approved of mob violence. Just one time when God said, *Okay, this time circumstances justify ignoring the laws.* Well, if it's there, I couldn't find it, folks. But I did come upon one reference to a mob, a very famous reference, that I'm sure you'll recognize. It took place in the Garden of Gethsemane. *'While He was still speaking,'* Luke tells us, *'suddenly a mob was there, and one of the Twelve named Judas was leading them. He came near Jesus to kiss him.'*"

CHAPTER 19

Josh closed the service with a prayer, this time asking the Lord to grant the men of Whitegrass the strength to control their passions. Just as Jesus, on the cross, refused to succumb to hatred—of the Romans who crucified him or the Pharisees who betrayed him or the horde that chose Barabbas—the people of Whitegrass, no matter how outraged, must put their anger to the side. After all, even Jesus received a trial, as did Peter and Paul, though both were martyred. Surely, the man locked up in Sheriff Schofield's jail deserved the same.

Though he was anxious to get outside before his congregants dispersed, Josh went first to Sarah and Rachel. Carmelita had already left the church, probably to resume her place on the Nortons' buggy.

Josh took Rachel's hands between his own as Sarah kissed his cheek. He searched for words, found none, but then was pardoned as Rachel looked down at little Eli's sleeping face and said, "We're holding our own, Josh. And just so you know, you were inspiring. Elijah would have been proud to hear that sermon."

Sarah took her husband's hand. She looked into his reddening face for just a moment, amused in that way only women can be amused at his reaction to the compliment. Normally, they'd have discussed the sermon beforehand, but there'd been no time. "You did right, husband," she said. "Some things have to be."

Josh hurried outside, where he found Clancy King in a heated conversation with the owner of the Bright Chance Hotel, Smitty Wright. Clancy was the town's farrier. He cared for the hooves of the many horses owned by ranches scattered across a hundred square miles. Clancy's voice was raised, and he had a finger pointing at Smitty's chest. But if Smitty was intimidated, he didn't show a sign of it to Josh. Though well into his fifties, Smitty stood ramrod straight, his curled upper lip expressing his disdain. Clancy's living depended almost entirely on the patronage of ranchers like Uriah Thorpe, whose remuda included two hundred horses.

Uriah, for his part, sat astride his horse only a few yards away, the cowboy he'd brought to church alongside him on a chestnut stallion. Sam Graves, owner of the town's hardware store, and Charlie Drake, owner of the lumberyard, were also present.

The dispute between the two men had come down to Clancy sighting the biblical reference of "an eye for an eye" as a justification for lynching Francisco. Josh never learned what response Smitty might have made because the conversation stopped when Josh stepped through the door. Naturally, as church pastor, he was expected to address the issue. Josh had been hoping the eye-for-an-eye quote would be raised while the service was in progress, but this would have to do.

"Tell me, Clancy, what exactly do you make of that quote?" Josh asked.

"Believe it's the Lord's instructions to His people." Clancy pointed to a wagon with a sign fastened to its frame: PECOS FARRIER SERVICE. "I carry the Good Book everywhere I get myself to, just like my daddy told me. Ain't never leave it behind, Reverend. The way I view the matter, the Lord is tellin' us, plain as day, to get that Mexican and give 'im what he give to Elijah Norton."

"And that's what you want to do?"

"Yes sir, an eye for an eye. The Mexican's life for Elijah's."

"I see." Josh stepped close to the farrier, close enough to capture the man's full attention. "Now, if I could prove to you that the Bible quote, an eye for an eye, is not meant for you, would you change your mind about lynching Francisco Rivera?" When Clancy hesitated, Josh continued. "I don't believe you will, Clancy, but I'll make my point anyway. The phrase you cite, an eye for an eye, is found in Exodus and Leviticus. Far from a lynching license meant for individuals, the phrase is part of a longer set of instructions for judges. Do you get it, Clancy? For judges, not for you. So, does that change your mind?"

A voice came from behind, yet Josh had no difficulty identifying the speaker: Uriah Thorpe.

"You sure do have an oratorical gift, Reverend Hill," he said, his fake drawl especially apparent. "You talk real plain, but you got your mind wrapped around every word. Have to give you credit." Uriah tipped his hat, a spanking new Stetson. "Morning, Mrs. Norton. Please accept my condolences once again. And good morning to you as well, Mrs. Hill. I was just speaking to your husband's way with words."

Sarah and Rachel had come out of the church to stand beside Josh. He thought, for a moment, that Rachel was about to speak, but then a horse and rider, the horse going at a full gallop, rounded the church. The rider, a young cowboy with a raised scar above his lip, pulled to a halt in front of Uriah. He said nothing for a moment, as winded as the animal he rode, but then blurted out, "It's just like you said, Mr. Thorpe. Don Diego's brought his vaqueros to La Cantina."

"How many, Hack?"

"I counted twenty, sir."

Uriah straightened in the saddle. "Good job, boy. Now go on back there and keep an eye out. They move, you let me know. I'll be at the Red River."

Uriah looked over at Josh, but the preacher's eyes had turned to the man he supposed to be Cole Bradhurst. Josh was correcting an error in judgment. He'd taken the expression on Cole's face to be one of innocence, feigned or not, but he'd been wrong. Cole was merely indifferent. He had the look of veteran officers Josh had known during the war, men who sent other men to march across open fields.

"Reverend, Mrs. Hill, Mrs. Norton," Uriah said. "I bid you good afternoon."

The younger man beside him, though he didn't speak, also raised his hat, his eyes fixed on Reverend Hill. Josh responded with a nod. "Good afternoon to you, Cole." The man reacted, not with anger and not with surprise. Instead he smiled a delighted smile that Josh associated with a young child.

CHAPTER 20

Cole sat behind the reins of Uriah's open carriage, a beautifully appointed phaeton that might have belonged to the wealthiest planter in Charleston. The seats were of tufted leather, the floorboards of mahogany, the appointments gold-plated silver. The only missing item was a liveried black coachman. Instead, Thorpe had settled for his hired gun. Much safer that way.

They were en route, Uriah in back and Cole in front, to the Norton farm, coming from the Red River Saloon where they'd conferenced with their supporters through the late morning and early afternoon. Both men wore the same dark suits they'd worn to church, though Cole had chosen a string tie held together by a turquoise slide, while his boss sported a bright red ascot.

Uriah's buoyant mood was evident. The man couldn't stop talking. First thing after learning that Don Diego's vaqueros were at La Cantina, he'd sent off telegrams to Governor Davis and the state's two senators in Washington—James Flanagan and Morgan Hamilton. Don Diego, he informed the three men, was leading an active rebellion against law and order; he'd amassed a small army, his purpose to free a man lawfully detained on a charge of murder. The town of Whitegrass therefore needed immediate assistance. Governor Davis was asked to declare a state of emergency and call out the militia. The senators were asked to intervene with President Grant. Fort Baxter was only sixty miles away. Why not send out the cavalry?

"Course," Uriah explained as the phaeton bounced over the ruts, "ain't no way our governor can snap his fingers and call out the militia. Washington's even worse. Takes forever to do anything."

Cole looked across the scrubland at three separate storms, each pouring down rain on some distant stretch of ground. He'd begun to think, off and on, about how easy it would be to kill Uriah, how easy and how much pleasure it would give him. He wouldn't for two reasons. First, because he needed Uriah's money. Second, because a reputation for murdering employers would be sure to dim his future prospects.

"That's to the good, Cole," Uriah explained. "La Cantina's outside the town limits. It's used by the Mexicans, same as the Red River's used by whites. Who's to say the Mex's vaqueros ain't there to indulge themselves. No, the thing we have to do now is lure them vaqueros into Whitegrass. That's an invasion— of Texas by Mexico is how they'll see it in Washington and Austin. After that, it'll be *adiós*, Don Diego. If he don't run back to Mexico, he'll find himself hangin' from the branch of a tree."

Cole kept one eye on a storm to the west, its obsidian clouds seeming at war with the summertime-blue skies that surrounded them. Lightning poured down, along with the rain, and it was coming right at the phaeton, which suddenly seemed very small, a speck. Cole gave the reins a shake, and the black gelding broke into a well-practiced trot.

Uriah didn't speak again until the Norton farm came into view. The storm, by then, had broken into a thousand pieces before vanishing.

"Hired me some twenty new men. Rebel vets, or so they claim. I want you to look them over, Cole, decide which ones can take discipline. You'll have to train 'em up."

"For what, Mr. Thorpe?"

"For whatever comes next."

Though Cole could see Rachel in a field a hundred yards distant, he drove, at Uriah's direction, up to the hitching post in front of the house. Sarah was in the field as well, along with Carmelita and two Mexican fieldworkers, experienced by the look of them. Cole watched Sarah and Rachel confer, their conversation seeming animated. Then both women walked across the field to the house. Uriah was out of the carriage by then, his Stetson in his hand.

Cole remained where he was as Rachel approached. Her eyes passed over him without a hint of recognition. So much the better. When the stagecoach came through two days before, with Cole trailing behind, Rachel had come running out of the house with the news that her husband had been attacked. The stage's driver, Buck Rawling, had gone inside immediately, but Cole had remained in the yard.

Still mounted, Cole could hear his boss's voice, but not that of Rachel, who stood with her back to him. Sarah never spoke.

"Mrs. Norton," Uriah said, "I know this ain't the proper time for business, what with your husband only just in the ground. But if I'm the first to visit, I won't be the last." Uriah nodded several times, then glanced at the door of the house. He expected to be invited inside, but whatever Rachel told him didn't include an invitation.

"Well, seein' as you're busy, I'll state the nature of my errand. I've had an eye on your property for a long time, as you know. I've made several proposals in the past. Now I figure, what with all the circumstances, you should be ready to accept a reasonable offer."

Cole detected a note of anger in Uriah's tone. The man was accustomed to deference, in fact expected his orders to be done every minute of the day. Now Rachel wouldn't invite him into her home. This was lowly Rachel, wearing a sweat-soaked canvas apron over her sweat-soaked white dress, her hair a tangled mess, hands on her hips, her child behind her in a hammock suspended from the branch of a live oak.

"All right, the farm's not for sale," Uriah said. "You still believe you can salvage this crop, though it's turning bad before your eyes. That's natural. But I'll leave my offer on the table, exactly half what I offered the last time I was here. This ain't a profit-makin' operation any more. And by the way, as long as we're being rude, I'm making plans to buy up the loan your husband took at the First National in Dallas. I will soon hold the mortgage on this property."

Cole brought his fingertips to his pistol, just brushing the grip. He felt, at that moment, an immense sympathy for the woman whose husband he'd murdered, though he couldn't have said why. In his world, the world he'd chosen after the war, the strong eat the weak and there remained nothing more to be said on the subject.

Uriah shook his head as Rachel spoke, his mouth gradually expanding into a smirk. "This here is rough country still," he finally said. "Ain't like it's gonna be when the railroad comes through and the army finally exterminates the savages. No, ma'am, for right now the Comanches and Apaches run about wherever they've a mind to." Uriah settled his hat on his head. "Fact of the matter, Mrs. Norton, there's every kind of evil roams the plains on dark nights, including white men who ain't no better than Comanches. And here you are, out here alone, with a little baby who still needs you. Don't make a whole lotta sense to a man like me, but you do as you please, Mrs. Norton, because it's my belief that I'll have the property one way or the other. If I can't buy it, I'll eventually foreclose. That's because you still need someone to buy your crop, even if you manage to get it in. That someone, I can promise you, will not be me."

CHAPTER 21

Josh rode out to the Norton ranch later that afternoon. The skies by then were fully overcast, bringing the temperature down, and he was able to push Sunset a bit harder. His thoughts, as he rode, were of a town council meeting that had transpired in Pace Granger's office on the first floor of the lawyer's home. There were eight men there, including Josh, an invitee. All agreed that Uriah intended to provoke Don Diego and that his plans went far beyond Francisco Rivera. Uriah Thorpe wanted a war.

What to do about it? No one among the businessmen at the meeting had an answer. Worse, Judah Burke was on the council and continually urged the men to do nothing, to look away, to let events play out. The war would come. It was inevitable; if not now, then later on. America for Americans. Mexico for Mexicans.

"The Mexicans have a country for themselves," he'd insisted. "It's time we did too."

Josh suspected that others on the council, including Charlie Drake and Sam Graves, owners of the lumberyard and the hardware store, shared Judah's sentiments. The only problem was the timing. What with the railroad holding the fate of Whitegrass in its hands, a range war just wouldn't do.

Uriah, Josh realized as he absorbed the back-and-forth, didn't care about Whitegrass. At present, the rancher was driving his cows more than two hundred miles into Nebraska along the Chisolm Trail. A detour to Fort Baxter, sixty miles away, would be a relatively minor inconvenience, especially if it meant eliminating Don Diego's presence on the range.

***

Josh turned down the brim of his hat as it began to drizzle. He urged Sunset into a canter, much against the horse's will. Twenty minutes later, he reached the farm where he found Rachel, Sarah, and Carmelita in the barn. Carmelita was milking the farm's only cow, while Rachel tried, unsuccessfully, to dose her ailing mule with a remedy for its colic. Sarah was sitting on a stool nearby, holding little Eli while she examined the blisters on her hands.

"I tried to convince your stubborn wife to wear gloves," Rachel said, "but she wouldn't listen. I have a treatment, though. Learned it from a squaw, an Apache who started out working for Elijah's daddy. Made from prickly pear."

Josh stepped up to the mule and held its head still while Rachel pushed the medication far down the animal's throat, forcing it to swallow. Then he took Rachel's hands—noting how rough they were, the hands of a woman living close to the earth—and stared into her eyes for a moment.

"Do not be afraid, pastor." The accented voice belonged to Carmelita. "She is a woman. She will go on."

"Fortitude comes from the Lord," he said. "It flows from the God we pray to for the strength to endure hardship. We must never forget that despair is the greatest of Satan's tools. But I don't find despair in you, Rachel. I find you as brave as any soldier marching into battle."

Rachel shook her head, the message obscure to Josh, before leading the mule to a stall. "Uriah Thorpe was out here this afternoon," she said. "He made me an offer on the farm, half what he offered the last time. Had somebody with him, too. I didn't let on, but it was the same cowboy who rode in with the stage. Only this time he wore a suit and had a pistol strapped to his hip."

"Cole Bradhurst," Josh said. "He's Uriah's hired gun."

It was Sarah who spoke first. "Do you think he had something to do with . . ."

"Thinking is one thing; proving is another." Josh went on to describe the council meeting. "Aside from the few of us, I've yet to find anyone who believes Francisco innocent. The only issue is whether he should or shouldn't have a trial. Hanging is the expected end of either course."

With the afternoon wearing down, Josh headed out to the river, the main reason he'd come to the farm. One question had intrigued him from the beginning, the objection raised by Sheriff Schofield. If someone besides Francisco had attacked Elijah Norton, where had he gone after the attack? Common sense led you to believe that he'd put as much distance between himself and his victim as he could. But common sense also told you that soldiers wouldn't march across an open field into massed cannon fire. Only they did. They marched across open fields in the face of murderous fire and commonly won the ground.

Cole was a professional, Josh finally decided, and no professional would have attacked Elijah without having his retreat carefully planned. The mule deer strapped to the man's horse was proof positive that he'd come with a well-developed strategy.

Josh scanned the scrubland beyond the Pecos River, only to find that nothing had changed since the last time he'd stood on this spot. The open prairie offered no obvious hiding place for miles in any direction. Cole couldn't have ridden away. Therefore, he must have retreated to a nearby place of concealment. There was, to Josh's way of thinking at that moment, no third possibility.

That left the narrow strips of greenery bordering either side of the river. Josh examined each bank carefully. The trees and brush along the near side were thinner and clearly visible from the house. On the far side, the banks were steeper and wider away from the ford. As he had earlier, Josh identified small stands of cottonwood, desert willow, and buckeye, along with brush that rose in places to the height of a man's chest.

Josh mounted Sunset and urged him into the river. Like most of the rivers in West Texas, the Pecos was fed with snowmelt from mountains in New Mexico. Now, in late July, the muddy water moved sluggishly, the current barely detectable. It rose only to Sunset's knees and hocks, and the horse had no trouble pushing through. Josh paused before the far bank, allowing the horse to drink while he looked north and south, evaluating the terrain as he often had while still a soldier. The question was simple enough. Which way had Cole gone after he crossed the river? Not south, surely. That would have taken him past the house. True, the cover was exceptionally thick, but why take the risk when he could travel north, keeping the barn between himself and the house, for a least five hundred yards?

As he imagined the sequence, Josh stroked Sunset's powerful neck. Cole would have seen Elijah working in the corral and the barn behind him as he crossed the river. More than likely, he would have examined the fields as well. But he wouldn't have seen Francisco, who was working in a field below the house. Again, as a professional, he would know he had a perfect opportunity to carry out what must have been Uriah Thorpe's orders. To carry out Uriah's orders and still make his escape.

Josh urged Sunset forward as he revised his opinion. More than likely, Cole had evaluated the conditions before he broke cover, before he even started across the river. Before he mounted up, he knew that Elijah—a simple farmer repairing a corral fence—was at his mercy.

Thirty yards upriver, Josh came upon the clear prints of a horse's hooves in a patch of muddy soil, prints that disappeared in a rocky patch thirty yards later. By then, Josh already had his eye on a dense stand of cottonwood saplings ringing a larger tree, the whole surrounded by desert sage and mesquite.

Josh led Sunset to the edge of the brush, then dismounted, leaving the horse to nibble the grasses. Sunset wasn't much to look at, but he was faithful and patient. He wouldn't go anywhere.

On foot, Josh circled the stand, looking for a break in the cover. He found it to the northeast, a clear path marked by hoofprints that led into a small, well-trodden clearing. A pile of relatively fresh dung marked one edge, while the stump of a cigar, still moist in the center, proved that the animal had been accompanied by a human being. Josh couldn't prove that Cole had smoked that cigar and he knew it. Nevertheless, beyond any doubt he could muster, he knew that Francisco was innocent.

Josh laughed to himself. Stay out of town affairs? Avoid taking sides? Remain neutral? Well, it had seemed like a good idea at the time.

***

After making his goodbyes to Rachel and Sarah, Josh led Carmelita out onto the porch. "I don't know any good way to say this, but . . ."

Carmelita's tiny smile brought the pastor to a halt. He'd come to believe there were times when the woman spoke to some knowledge beyond his grasp.

"You want to know about Cole Bradhurst. If I had business with him, yes? At the Red River?"

"I want to know who I'm dealing with. If you can help me . . ."

Carmelita brought her finger to her lips. "The man has a liking for blondes, a little bit heavy. I never went with him. But I have seen men like him many times in my life, the ones who speak little, who live inside themselves. I am also meeting in my life very dangerous men who are opposite to Cole. These men are laughing and drinking and dancing. Happy, yes? For at least this time in the Red River Saloon. But men like Cole are never happy. They are lost men. They look for something they cannot even name."

CHAPTER 22

Josh was still a mile from town when the rain picked up. He merely hunched his shoulders for a few minutes, hoping it would slacken. Big mistake, because it suddenly began to pour. Josh was pretty much drenched by the time he got to the slicker in his saddle bags, and wetter still by the time he buttoned it over his chest. This wasn't an angry storm, spitting lightning and thunder, like most he'd witnessed in the past few days. The clouds overhead were the color of flint and spread as far as he could see in every direction. It would rain for hours, obliterating the hoofprints leading to and inside the little clearing. The dung and cigar would be wet, soggy messes that might have been deposited a few days ago, or a few weeks ago. As evidence, they were valueless.

There were times, and this was one of them, when Josh wished he'd never been a town marshal, that he knew nothing about evidence, that he'd never seen a killer go free. But hard-acquired knowledge can't be erased and being a marshal in a mining town is about as hard as it gets. There'd be no presumption of innocence here. Pace Granger, as Francisco's lawyer, would have to prove his client innocent, and that would take evidence that, even as Josh approached the jail, was being destroyed.

The jail in Whitegrass wasn't much to look at, inside or out. It differed from most of the town's serviceable architecture only in that it was constructed of mud brick instead of wood. Inside, Sheriff Schofield's office was limited to a single room with a pair of desks set apart from each other. Schofield sat on the edge of one of those desks. Behind him, a gun rack held a pair of shotguns and four Winchester repeating rifles. Two men sat beside the second desk, both armed. Josh recognized the men, Franz Weber and Gerhard Schneider, German immigrant-farmers who'd fled religious persecution in their home country. They were part of a fairly large community, these immigrants, and though ordinarily clannish, they did occasionally shop in Josh's store. He'd always found them to be steady, resolute, and devoted to the rule of law. They were proving it now.

"Trey, I need to speak with you." Josh glanced at the door leading to the cells at the back of the jail. Francisco would be confined in one of them, awaiting his fate. "Outside, if possible."

Sheriff Schofield took a moment to examine the rain still streaming from the edges of Josh's slicker. "On the porch? Or do we have to stand in the mud?"

"The porch'll do."

"You appear to be a bit on the grouchy side, Reverend. Mind tellin' me what's got up your drawers?"

"That's exactly what I intend to do, Trey."

A moment later, the two men stood on the porch, listening to the rain pound on the thin roof while they dodged several leaks. Schofield, as a matter of habit, scanned the street, slowing when he came to the Red River Saloon, then passing on. When he discovered no immediate threat, he again faced Josh.

"So, what can I do for you, Reverend?"

"Your theory," Josh said, "is all wrong."

"How so?" Schofield took the stump of a cigar from his pocket. He blew a bit of ash from the tip, then struck a match.

"You're convinced that no one could have gotten away before Rachel came out of the house. You're wrong."

Josh went on to describe his little journey, first across the Pecos, then upriver along the bank until he reached and explored the sheltered clearing. "Less than five minutes, Trey. That's how long it would take a man who knew where he was going. And something else, too. From behind the trees and the brush, in that little clearing, you can look out between the branches and see the corral. Elijah's killer watched Francisco enter the corral, followed by Rachel. He also watched them haul Elijah away. With nobody to witness his escape, he could take his time."

Sheriff Schofield wasn't a man to speak the first words that popped into his head. He looked down at his boots as he pushed his thumb against the side of a twisted nose broken many times. Finally, he raised his eyes and said, "I don't doubt your word, Reverend. Known you too long for that. But all you can really prove is that somebody was in that clearing at some time in the past. No way you can prove the man was in there on the afternoon Elijah was attacked."

"Can't even prove the first part, not anymore," Josh admitted. "The soil in the clearing is sandy enough to be pure mud by now. But the point is that someone else besides Francisco could have been there, which you've been claiming to disbelieve."

"Even if I agree—no, even if you could prove—that someone else *might* have committed this murder, it don't mean that someone else did. Rachel found Francisco kneeling beside her husband. His clothes was bloody and the murder weapon was layin' right at his feet. The man's got to stand trial, no two ways about it. You wanna help him, go talk to his lawyer."

"You're the sheriff, Trey. You're the man tasked with investigating." Josh's voice sharpened as he spoke, much against his will. "I know because I once did your job."

"I got me more than enough to do keepin' Francisco alive."

Josh nodded once. There was a limit to how far Sheriff Schofield would go in opposing Uriah Thorpe. "All right, I'll talk to Pace. But I've got one more question I'd like you to answer. And bein' as you've had Francisco for company these past two days, I think you're in the best position to answer truly. Do you think Francisco Rivera murdered Elijah Norton?"

"No."

"So, what are you doing to see that an innocent man isn't hung for another man's crime?"

"That's two questions, Reverend. One too many."

CHAPTER 23

Pace Granger wasn't in his office when Josh walked through the door. He was in the back of the house with his oldest son, Robert, taking up a large rug that Mary Ellen intended to beat on the following morning if the sun came out. The lawyer only responded when Josh called his name twice, the second time loud enough to be heard over the incessant rain.

"Hold your horses," Pace called. A moment later, his hair speckled with dust, he strode into his office. "Ah, Reverend Hill. Dripping all over my floor."

"Sorry about that, Pace. Got caught in the rain on my way back from the Norton farm."

"How's Rachel bearing up?"

"Rachel is a frontier woman. She won't fold, no matter how bad she's hurting. But she's got help now."

"That woman, Carmelita?"

"Yes, her. She's proved herself rock solid."

"Excellent. Anyway, I'm glad you stopped over because there's something I want to talk about, a proposal. Now I won't have to go out in the rain to find you."

Josh managed a dutiful chuckle, then motioned for Pace to continue. "Let's hear it."

"All right, I spoke to Charlie Drake and Sam Graves a couple of hours ago. We've come up with an idea and I'd like you to listen to it. Are you still friendly with Padre Pilar?"

"We say hello to one another, if you call that friendly."

"I'm sure this won't come as any surprise, but the way we evaluate the situation, there's a range war coming with two men leading the way. The man we know, Uriah Thorpe, can't be reached. He's the one starting the war. But what about the man we don't know? What about Don Diego? Can he be reasoned with?"

Josh looked down at the puddle accumulating around his boots. Mary Ellen would not be happy. "I have no idea, Pace. Never met the man."

"Nor I. But every Sabbath, Don Diego attends Mass at Padre Pilar's church. The two men have to know each other, so it's just possible that you can reach Don Diego through the Padre. Maybe we can head the war off before it gets started."

"You want me to approach Don Diego?"

"Who else, Reverend? Who else would Padre Pilar listen to?"

A peace mission? A mission without conflicts? Josh felt suddenly cheered. Yes, of course, he would. As the town pastor, he was more or less obligated to prevent violence whenever he could. Not that he expected much. The descendent of Spanish aristocrats, Don Diego was known to be a proud man, deeply concerned with his personal honor and committed to the Mexicans in West Texas. He was their collective godfather, their protector, and that included Francisco Rivera.

"Okay, Pace, I'll stop by the mission tomorrow. Hopefully, Padre Pilar will be receptive. But that's not why I'm here. I crossed the river this afternoon before the rain started and did some exploring."

As he had with Sheriff Schofield, Josh went on to describe, in detail, what he'd discovered. When he finished, Pace asked an obvious question. "Have you spoken to the sheriff?"

"I have, Pace, and I wouldn't expect much help from that quarter. Trey's determined to protect his prisoner, but that's as far as he's prepared to go. And what I found in that copse, it's not evidence anymore, not with it raining this hard."

Pace walked over to his desk. He sorted through the messy papers covering the top until he found what he wanted. "This here," he told Josh, "is a copy of a telegram I sent out this afternoon. That cowboy . . . no, not a cowboy, not by a long shot. That gunslinger, Cole Bradhurst? It's true that he rode onto the Norton farm in the company of the stagecoach, but that doesn't prove anything." Pace rattled the single sheet he held. "This telegram is addressed to Buck Rawling. You know Buck, right?"

Josh nodded. Buck Rawling was the stage driver on a route that began in Austin, then cut a long loop through a number of towns on the way to Whitegrass. From Whitegrass, it headed north to Fort Baxter before starting the long journey back to Austin.

"I'm trying to find out just when Bradhurst joined the stage," Pace continued. "A mile out? Two? Ten? If you're right, Bradhurst was on the wrong side of the river. He'd have to cross the Pecos in order to get back to the ranch. When he did, there was a chance he'd be spotted. The stagecoach gave him cover. But if he only joined the stage a few miles from the farm, I've got a right to ask him what he was doing before that time."

Josh absorbed the smooth and confident tone, but he wasn't fooled. Cole had ridden onto the farm with a freshly killed mule deer strapped to his horse. He'd prepared his story in advance.

"Tell me the honest truth," Josh asked the lawyer. "Does Francisco have any chance at trial?"

Pace looked away for a moment. "I'm going to ride out to Rachel's farm tomorrow morning. I'll inspect your clearing while I'm there."

"Look for a large cottonwood surrounded by saplings and brush. The entrance is from the back."

"I'll do that, but I've got another reason for going. This one's more delicate. If Rachel is willing to testify in Francisco's defense, as a character witness, it would go a long way toward convincing a jury that he might actually be innocent. The way it is now, the whole town thinks he's guilty."

"And you believe that Rachel is enough to change those opinions?"

Pace didn't answer directly, nor did he meet Josh's eyes. "I'm a lawyer," he said. "I provide the best defense I can. Sometimes it's good enough, sometimes it's not."

***

Two hours later, Josh stood in front of his store as arriving cowboys hitched their ponies to posts up and down main street. He watched the cowboys slog through the mud on the unpaved street, the heels of their boots sinking out of sight, then climb to the raised wooden boardwalk. The rain had stopped and the atmosphere seemed almost festive. As if these young men, still sober, wanted no more than a night on the town. As if they weren't bent on murder, as if this weren't the Sabbath.

Josh remembered what he had told Rachel and Carmelita about despair. There existed, in his mind, no greater cause of despair than human beings themselves. The cowboys joked as they went, laughing and hooting, taking joy in what they hoped to do that night. Were they worthy of redemption? Was he? Was any human being?

You're commanded to resist these thoughts, Josh told himself. As you're commanded to resist the temptations of the flesh. You're commanded to close all those doors leading into the human heart, leaving only one open, an entrance for charity, for the love of others, for the eternal love of the Lord. But there were times when it was hard to see any good in people, when questions seeped in, questions that wouldn't go away. Like why would the great God, the creator of a universe that included more stars than a man could count in a lifetime, bother with people at all?

"Reverend, is the store still open?"

Startled, Josh turned to find himself staring into the eyes of a woman named Bertha. Just that, a first name only. Bertha plied her ancient trade at the Red River Saloon, and like most of her sisters, she shopped at Whitegrass Mercantile.

"I need me some red silk, if you got it," she explained. "Gonna dress up special for the celebration. Old Uriah told me every cowboy in town would have money in their pockets after they come back from hangin' the Mexican that murdered Elijah Norton."

CHAPTER 24

For Cole, the fight to come was, first and foremost, about survival. And there was sure to be a fight. Cole knew that because Uriah was nowhere to be found. He'd left Yancey Jackson to inspire the boys, as he'd left Cole with specific instructions. Don Diego would bring his vaqueros into Whitegrass within a day, two at the most. The fight needed to happen tonight, and Cole was to make sure it happened.

It would, Uriah insisted, take only one shot to set the whole thing off.

"I don't want you to be taking that shot, Cole," Uriah had instructed. "The preacher's been talkin' you up to anybody willing to listen. Way I see it, you're likely to be watched."

Cole recalled the conversation word for word. Uriah had taken his hired gun to task for crossing the river with the stagecoach, but Cole believed that he'd had no choice. He couldn't know that Francisco would become a suspect, much less be arrested. No, he was only sure that Sheriff Schofield would be summoned to the Norton farm, probably in the company of his deputy and the town doctor. Sheriff Schofield was no fool. If he and his deputy decided to explore the far side of the river, the resulting fight would be to the death.

The dust trail thrown up by the stagecoach had been visible while the stage was still several miles out. By then, Elijah had already been inside the house, tended by his wife and the field hand. Cole had seen his chance and he hadn't hesitated. He'd taken a circuitous route that intersected with the oncoming stage a mile from the Pecos River. As far as he could tell, the stunt had worked, at least until Reverend Hill decided to interest himself in an affair that was none of his business.

***

"Now, boys," Yancey proclaimed, "there are times in life when a man is called to take a stand. Times when his mettle's put to the test. Don't care how easygoing he might be, how friendly, how mild. When the enemy is at the gate, patriots seize their weapons and prepare for battle. And here we are right now, boys, with the enemy no more than a few miles outside Whitegrass, preparin' to ravage our little town." Yancey raised a finger. "Don't trick yourselves into thinkin' those vaqueros, bloodthirsty as any savage on the prairie, will satisfy themselves with protectin' that killer, or even with breakin' him out of Sheriff Schofield's jail. Once a Mex tastes blood, there's no stoppin' 'em, not until they've killed every man and burned every building and defiled every woman they can get their hands on. They proved that at the Alamo and a dozen other battles. No quarter, if you remember. Kill everyone."

As Yancey continued, his oratory growing ever more inflammatory, Cole signaled to Stoney Greene, the bartender. Stoney poured Cole a shot of whiskey imported from far-off Kentucky, which Cole swallowed in a single gulp. Ordinarily, Cole didn't drink before going into battle. This time was different. This time he offered a silent toast.

Lambs to the slaughter, he said to himself. Lambs to the slaughter. Uriah's promised soldiers had yet to arrive, and these half-drunk kids were ill-prepared for what was about to happen. If Cole let it happen.

Cole left Yancey to his pep talk. He walked out of the saloon and onto the boardwalk. The storm that had soaked Whitegrass only a few hours before was now little more than a few ragged clouds arranged like claws across a star-studded sky. A waxing moon stood on end at the horizon, seeming a million miles away and thin as a sickle. The unlit torches awaited to Cole's right. The Winchesters were neatly stacked to his left.

Who had paid for them, Cole asked himself. Relatively new to the market, Winchesters sold for fifty dollars each, a price way beyond the means of the average, underpaid cowboy. Yet someone must have purchased them, that someone being Uriah. And that led to another question, and another and another. First, how long had Uriah been planning this war? Second, had he bought the Winchesters months ago and all this time been waiting for an excuse? Third and most important, who and how many would he sacrifice to satisfy his ambitions?

Cole glanced past the hardware store across the street. George Thompson was out there somewhere, a buffalo robe pulled over his shoulders. The rifle alongside him wouldn't be a Winchester. George favored a Spencer with a telescopic sight, as did many of the buffalo hunters working the Texas prairies. The weapon's .52 caliber rounds packed enough force to bring down the largest bulls.

With the street still deserted, George would be tugging on whatever whiskey he'd brought along. There was no stopping the man. But the alcohol wouldn't affect his aim. When Cole raised his hat, George would fire a single round into the body of a defender unlucky enough to be in his line of sight. The survivors were certain to respond. The war would begin.

Cole's thoughts were interrupted by the sound of boots on the wooden boardwalk. He turned to discover the preacher, Reverend . . . It came to him after moment, Reverend Hill, headed right for him. Despite the preacher being unarmed, Cole's hand instinctively moved toward the ivory grips of his Colt.

"Mr. Bradhurst," the preacher said, his eyes boring into Cole's. "Good evening."

If asked only a few seconds before, Cole would have insisted that he feared no man. Now he found himself relieved when Hill passed him by to enter the saloon. The preacher advanced only a few steps past the swinging doors, but that was enough. Yancey's speech ended abruptly and the mob quieted.

"I'm going to keep this short, men," Reverend Hill said, his voice booming out to cover the entire room. "If you do this thing, if you commit this murder, the God who judges all will hold you accountable, be you a leader or a follower. Some judgments cannot be escaped."

Cole smiled in admiration when the preacher turned on his heel and walked out of the saloon. Know when to advance, know when to retreat. But the gunman's attitude reversed completely when the reverend stopped in front of him. The two men were almost the same height, and now they stared into each other's eyes. The preacher's, Cole decided, were entirely unafraid, as if he'd already determined what lay at Cole Bradhurst's core, as if he'd reached to the very bottom, as if what he found didn't frighten him in the slightest.

"Tell me, Mr. Bradhurst, which is the greater sin? To kill a man, or to let an innocent man hang for that killing?"

Cole had learned as a child to hold his anger in check. He held it in check now, standing face-to-face with a man who'd accused him of murder.

"Reverend Hill, did you fight in the war?" he asked.

"I did, Mr. Bradhurst."

"Lotta casualties in wartime, Reverend. Folks dyin' everywhere you look. The good, the bad, the innocent, the guilty." Cole paused for a moment but didn't drop his eyes. "There's a new war comin', comin' right here to Whitegrass, Texas. Bein' as you're customarily unarmed, I believe it would be a good idea if you were to avoid the line of fire."

The preacher said nothing, merely tipping his hat as he turned to go. But Cole wasn't through. "One more thing, Reverend."

"And what's that?"

"No need to be formal. You can call me Cole."

"Well, Cole, here's something to consider. There was a time, before Jesus came into the world, that the sins you and I have committed could not be forgiven, a time when the sin of Adam still clung to us. That changed after Jesus shed His blood, when He gave his life for all mankind. That includes you, Cole, just so you understand. You can tell yourself that it's too late, that you've gone too far. That's what I told myself for many years. But it's not true. Redemption is always close at hand. You've only to open your heart to God, and He will comfort you."

Cole watched the reverend walk back the way he'd come for a few seconds, then put the man out of his mind. An element had been added to the cheers coming from inside the Red River. The hands were laughing now, undoubtedly at the reverend's expense, undoubtedly urged on by Yancey.

The preacher had accomplished nothing. The lambs would go forward.

A few minutes later, as if to prove the point, the mob spewed through the Red River's swinging doors, grabbing torches and rifles as they came. One torch was lit, its fire passed to another and another, until the collective blaze flared in every shop window on main street. Cole stayed well off to the side as the mob advanced toward the jail, waving their rifles and torches in the air. As proof of their unreasoning state, they began singing Dixie. Were they even aware of the mud that pulled at the heels of their boots? Of how they slipped every time they took a forward step? Were they aware, even to the smallest degree, of what the immediate future held for them?

The mob's progress was relatively slow. The wet street, slick with the waste deposited by thousands of horses in the nine months since it had last rained, made every step hazardous. But again, spurred on by alcohol and passion, a deadly combination in Cole's experience, the cowboys took no notice, their slips and slides producing only delighted guffaws. Perhaps their numbers had made them reckless. Fifty men, well-armed, marching against seven. Their attitude projected a confidence that no amount of reason could dent.

That would change, and soon. Once they cleared the cistern, Cole would signal George Thompson by raising his hat. Thompson would fire the Spencer within seconds, taking down one of the seven defenders. The survivors would open up, also within seconds, the shotguns first, then the Winchesters, shot after shot into enemies who could barely stand, who knew nothing of organized retreat.

Lambs to the slaughter. Lambs who'd mistaken themselves for wolves.

Suddenly Cole realized that Uriah never meant for the attack to succeed, that he wanted Francisco to remain safe in that jail, for Don Diego to bring his vaqueros into Whitegrass. With the two sides facing off, Governor Davis would have to act.

Cole shook his head, as if to rid his ear of a stray insect, but the insight wouldn't go away.

For what seemed to him a long time, mesmerized by the raucous cheers and the flaming torches, Cole didn't move, not at all. As a soldier, he'd hated Ulysses Grant, a man whose army could suffer ten thousand casualties on Tuesday and attack again on Wednesday. Never mind the widows and fatherless children, the young lives cut short, Grant knew he'd win the war if he kept at it. Now Cole was called upon to give the signal, to order the charge, knowing tonight's lost battle would herald a victory down the line.

Cole raised his hand to his flat-crowned hat and lifted it, not far, but enough to alert George. As Cole had predicted, a shot ran out only a second or two later.

The round struck Schofield's deputy, Hank Potter, on the left side. He staggered back but did not fall, instead firing both barrels of his shotgun, at head height, into the mob. Sheriff Schofield followed an instant later, again at head height, so that individual pellets were certain to strike men in the middle and the back of the tightly packed crowd. The cheers, the chorus of Dixie, stopped dead, replaced by the echo of the shotgun blasts and the screams of the wounded. The five defenders on the roof, already on one knee, fired into the crowd, each round seeming to find flesh.

The cowboys panicked, instantly and without returning fire. They followed their instincts as they turned and tried to run, sliding in the mud, tripping over fallen comrades, tossing their weapons to the side as Cole had seen defeated troops on the battlefield discard their own weapons. The wounded crawled on all fours, bodies smeared in a mix of mud and blood. One man, blinded, ran in circles until cut down by a bullet fired from the roof. Another rose to his knees, throat pulsing blood, and began to pray.

Still off to one side, Cole took cover in the alley running alongside the stables. He didn't fire his own weapon, didn't even draw the Colt. Uriah may have ordered a slaughter, but Cole didn't intend to be one of the slaughtered. The chaos on the street had taken him right back to the war. Cole had been only too willing to risk his life in the great cause, but there was nothing great about Uriah's naked ambition. By the time the battle was over . . .

War is chaos, as a commanding officer had once informed Cole. Always expect the unexpected. Sheriff Trey Schofield proved the adage true when he stepped into the street and raised his hand. Well-schooled, the men behind him ceased to fire, though they held their rifles at the ready. Only Schofield let the barrel of his weapon drop. The battle was over.

Sheriff Schofield's restless eyes darted across the battlefield, back and forth, back and forth, until they found Cole. A smile followed.

"Mr. Bradhurst," he called out, "would you be so kind as to fetch the doctor?"

CHAPTER 25

Three lay dead, including Deputy Hank Potter, and twelve injured, three of them critically. They lay, the living, on pallets in Josh and Sarah's little church, the largest open space available. Sarah was there, putting her wartime experience to good use. Sarah had been a nurse, working in field hospitals for the final year of the war. They were Union hospitals, not Rebel, but nobody cared on that morning. A wound cleaned and bandaged, a sip of water offered to a dying man, a comforting touch, the sound of a woman's voice . . . politics played no part in what Sarah and the other nurses had to offer. Sarah was toiling alongside Martha Robinson, wife to the town furniture maker and carpenter, and Babe White of the Red River Saloon. All three had extensive wartime experience, and they worked as a unit. Their nursing skills were readily apparent, as was the compassion that flowed from their hearts.

Josh felt the women move about him as he knelt beside a gutshot cowboy named Shane Vincent. Plain and simple, the boy was almost surely going to die. The bullet had entered the boy's abdomen on the right side and traveled all the way through. His organs could not have been spared.

No one had seen fit to inform Shane, not Doc Cassidy or the nurses. That task was left to Reverend Hill, an almost impossible task because Shane seemed not to recognize, much less accept, even the possibility of death. Despite the searing pain that doubled him up every few seconds.

"Think I'll get myself to home once I heal up," he told Josh through gritted teeth. "Ain't seen my momma in two years."

"And where is home, son?"

"Up to Nebraska. Plenty of work there when I was still growin', but . . ." The boy paused, his eyes squeezing shut. He held his breath for a moment, then leaned his head back and grinned at the preacher. "But that dang railroad come through and that was the end of the cattle drives. My older brothers was already growed and there wasn't no work for me, so I come south to Texas. But I'll be goin' home right enough. Soon's I heal."

Josh laid his hand on the boy's shoulder, as he'd seen chaplains do many times during the war. Shane was so young, a lad at the beginning of his adulthood, a boy who would never be a husband, never be a father. Josh's first instinct was to offer comfort, to tell the boy yes, you will see your mother again, you will hold her and hug her and shower her with kisses. But Shane had left the Red River Saloon with murder in his heart, and hell was forever; there was no time to waste. The boy was bleeding into his abdomen, his face growing more and more pale. He'd be unconscious before long.

"You need to get yourself right with the Lord, son," he said as gently as he could. "Will you pray with me?"

Josh watched Shane's blue eyes jerk back as though he'd come upon a scorpion in his boot. He held that pose for a moment, then touched his belly before raising his hand as if holding some rare object. Confused now, he simply stared at the blood dripping from his fingers.

"What we tried to do last night, Reverend," he finally muttered, "it was a sin, like you said in the saloon. Ain't that right?"

"It was, Shane."

"Reverend, I'm scared now."

"Then pray with me."

Josh led the boy in the Lord's prayer, phrase by phrase, slower than slow, hoping to let each word find its place in the boy's heart. But the terror that rose into Shane's eyes, though his mouth continued to move, to recite the words, only grew more intense.

"His hand is already outstretched," Josh said. "The hand you need to take."

The words were barely out of Josh's mouth when dark red blood, arterial blood, began to flow from both nostrils and the boy settled into a sleep from which he would never awaken. He couldn't have been more than seventeen.

***

Josh was outside an hour later, standing on his porch, exhausted. He'd moved from one wounded man to another, offering comfort, joining them in prayer. Now came the waiting part, the waiting and the hoping. Hoping the wound would heal, that no infection set in. One boy, a furrow across the left side of his head deep enough to reveal his skull, put it best. "If I develop the gangrene, Doc," he asked, "will y'all have to cut my head off?"

Once they realized the boy was joking, they'd shared a much-needed laugh, all of them, including Josh and Sarah. But the fear of gangrene was real. Josh had seen the mounds of amputated limbs behind field hospitals all across the south, and there was no shaking the images. Infections often presented a greater threat to life than the bullet that inflicted the wound.

Now they were at it again, no lessons learned, the suffering, the utter futility, the widows and the orphans. All those cowboys knew, when they had left the Red River Saloon, was to kill. If Schofield got out of the way, they would have settled for his prisoner. If not, they would have slaughtered him too. Worse still, they believed their actions to be righteous.

***

The day had turned hot, as July days in West Texas usually do, but an added element, a rare humidity, made the atmosphere even more uncomfortable. The clear skies proved nothing. Far beyond the river, two storms raced across the scrubland, dropping funnels of rain toward the parched earth. The random nature of these storms struck Josh, and he compared them, instinctively, to the storms that swept through the human heart. Blue skies that spread from horizon to horizon somehow produced clouds that boiled up toward the heavens, that spat rain and hail with the fury of a Gatling gun. Mobs formed as unpredictably, but once formed, they moved with a common fury that denied even the possibility of restraint.

Duty and obligation, along with a stubborn attitude that refused to surrender until all was lost, finally got Josh moving. His destination, when he set out, was Whitegrass's second church, Mission de Santa Maria, Pablo Pilar's domain. Josh tried to prepare himself, to fashion some sort of argument likely to convince Don Diego. Unfortunately, the simple truth couldn't be denied. If Don Diego didn't protect Francisco, he'd eventually be lynched, and Don Diego, after two attacks on the jail, had to know it. That transformed the town-elders' hope, that Don Diego could be convinced to back off, into a child's fantasy, a Christmas wish. Don Diego would protect his people, to save face if for no other reason. He couldn't show weakness.

Josh stepped onto the boardwalk to find Judah Burke approaching, not the man he wanted to see at that moment. Judah was too smart to take part in either of the attacks on the jail, but his attitude suffused every step and every bullet. Hank Potter had been Trey Schofield's deputy since Whitegrass had become big enough to have a sheriff. Now he lay dead, his wife a widow, his five children without a provider. The older boy, not yet fifteen, would have to go to work.

Judah didn't offer his hand. "S'pose you ain't heard the news. Wagon train got looted the other side of Kinsey. Headed for us, Reverend, with goods on board for Whitegrass Mercantile. For me, too, and just about every businessman in Whitegrass."

Wagon trains had been robbed before. This was nothing new for Josh. "What about the drivers and the guards?"

"All alive. Seems the horses were taken, and they were left to walk the twenty miles to Kinsey. Took 'em all day, but they made it. Told their tale, too. They were ambushed by twenty men as they come through a ravine up on the Mescalero range. Them highwaymen, Reverend, they spoke Spanish. Their saddles, their spurs, and the bridles on their horses were trimmed with silver. Ain't no doubt they were Mexicans."

"I suppose the word's all over town?"

"That it is. Charlie Drake lost a wagonload of pine boards meant for sale to Faro Lamb. Faro wants to expand his stable, but he's just gonna have to hold his horses." Judah hesitated long enough for Josh to realize that he'd made a joke. When Josh didn't laugh, didn't even smile, he shook his head. "Believe it or not, I like you, Reverend. I believe you to be an honest man, which is pretty rare in these parts. That's why I came to you, because you're honest. What's happenin' here, it can't be stopped."

"What about the railroad? If the Southern-Pacific doesn't come through Whitegrass, Charlie Drake stands to lose a lot more than a load of pine boards."

"The railroad ain't goin' nowhere but through our little town. Word's out, the army's movin' Fort Baxter west, to where the savages are concentrated. Won't be any more Fort Baxter after that. No town, anyway. Plus, we got a natural ford that'll serve to move cattle until there's a bridge built."

"How do you know this?"

"Uriah Thorpe's been in touch with the railroad people for six months."

The claim was worthless, at least in Josh's eyes, but that meant nothing. Most of the town's respectable types would believe it because they had no choice. The forces moving events were well beyond containment. Uriah's claim at least offered hope.

"Now, Reverend, believe it or not, I didn't come here to make your life miserable. Figure you got enough on your mind, what with the dead and wounded. No, I'm here, like I said, to pass a friendly word. Step away, leave the fate of Whitegrass to others. You got funerals to prepare and the injured to attend. Your own congregation, too. That oughta be enough, Reverend. It's gotta be."

"And your fate, Judah? Should I leave that to others?"

The words had no effect on Judah, who tipped his hat and continued on his way. Josh watched him for a moment, thinking it was all part of the game humans play. There were no atheists in Whitegrass, none willing to admit it anyway. All claimed to believe in God's commandments and a final judgment, yet they violated those commandments regularly. Ezekiel had spoken of it, Isaiah and Jeremiah, too, all making the identical observation: *"You have eyes, but you do not see."*

Josh was still lost in thought when the vaqueros rode into town. They rode in single file, perhaps twenty men, seeming quite ordinary, except for the sombreros, in their denim and twill pants, their flannel shirts. The tack on their horses, far from trimmed with silver buckles, might have belonged to any hardworking cowboy.

The man who led them sat upright in the saddle, staring straight ahead, his bearing military. Dressed in black, he presented an attitude somber enough to make his intentions clear. Several of the men behind him wore bandoliers of ammunition, but the only relief from their leader's grave aspect, worn around his throat, was a band of leather with a slice of sea-green turquoise at the center.

They walked their horses in from the north, the boardwalks filling as they came, every store emptying. This was Yancey's prediction come to life. By tonight, most families would be huddled together, a rifle at the ready. Would there be a battle, a final battle, with the fate of Whitegrass in the offing? Something as simple as a bullet finding its way into a bale of hay at the stables could ignite a fire that could consumed much of the town. There's no organizing a bucket brigade when bullets are flying in all directions.

The vaqueros continued on their way, looking neither right nor left until they reached the saddle-maker's shop. Pablo Sierra was a fourth-generation leather worker. In addition to saddles, his work included chaps, bridles, hand-tooled belts, holsters, and incredibly beautiful boots. The boots were especially prized, and every rancher for miles around had a pair. That would end now. Pablo had chosen sides.

The vaqueros dismounted, taking their time, and led their horses to a small corral behind Pablo's shop. They let some of the animals inside, hitching the rest to the corral's railing before a small group drew their rifles and took up positions in front of the store. They were now between the jail and the Red River Saloon.

The remainder tended the horses. They unsaddled their mounts first, then fetched water from the cistern and allowed the animals to drink. Their leader, the man in black, was the first and only man to enter the saddlery. He offered his back as he went inside, a deliberate provocation—shoot me if you dare.

"What do you bet, Reverend, that Uriah's already sending off a telegram to the governor?" The voice belonged to Pace, Francisco's lawyer. "What do you bet that Governor Davis responds? Everyone knows that Davis is heavily invested in Texas cattle."

"Are you inviting me to gamble, Pace? Are you putting my soul in jeopardy?"

The joke was feeble enough, and the lawyer responded with a small smile. "You been to the mission yet?" he asked.

"I'm headed there now."

"Good luck, Reverend. For you and for the town."

CHAPTER 26

Josh hadn't been inside a Catholic church in many years, not since before the war, and then only to attend the odd wedding or christening in nearby Maryland. The first thing that struck him, when he stepped into Mission de Santa Maria, was the cool air that filled the church. The mission's walls were of stucco and thick, the shuttered windows small, but set across from each other so as to let the night air into the church. The sensation as Josh stepped from the bright sun into the dim interior, as the sweat chilled on his body, was of entering a different realm. The statues of the Virgin and the saints, Jesus mounted on his cross, contributed to the overall effect, despite Josh's firm belief that praying to statues in the hope of some benefit was pure idolatry.

Statuary or not, the mission offered no challenge to the great cathedrals back East. Like his own church, the whole of it, including the altar, was contained in a single space, a perfect rectangle perhaps a hundred feet front to back. Josh searched the space, his eyes sweeping over several elderly women until he found Padre Pilar kneeling before a table holding dozens of candles in small red jars. The priest's hands were steepled against his chest. His head was bowed, his lips moving.

Josh was reluctant to interrupt, but in this case, he had no choice. He walked to the front of the church, touched the priest's shoulder, and said, "Padre, may I have a word with you?"

The priest looked up, his dark eyes sad. "Of course, Reverend Hill."

As they exited the little church, Josh took a last look inside. Catholics saw their churches as sanctuaries, a place to escape

life's cares, a place to contemplate the life to come. Josh felt that
now, even as the door closed behind him. He stepped into the
July sunlight and pointed to the vaqueros stationed in front of the
saddlery.

"Are you surprised to see them, Padre?"

"No, I have known this war was coming."

"It doesn't have to."

"And how will you prevent this thing when God has given
free will to His children who do not listen?"

Josh smiled. "We sinful Protestants have a saying, Padre. God
helps those who help themselves."

"You will help yourself, and God will also help you? This
is an arrangement of much convenience." The priest's fingers
reached down to touch the rope he wore around his waist in lieu
of a belt. "Is this also how Señor Thorpe is thinking? He is helping himself to all of West Texas. Is he also believing that God will
help him?"

"Thorpe's in love with mammon, Padre. Wealth and power
are the only gods he serves. But I'm not here as Uriah's mes-
senger." Josh gestured toward the businesses in front of them.
"Nobody wants a war. There's been enough bloodshed already.
But Thorpe's deaf to reason, or to his conscience, if he has one.
I'm hoping that Don Diego will listen to reason. I'm hoping you
can arrange a meeting."

The priest took his time, his eyes moving from the vaqueros,
to the sheriff and his deputies, to the cowboys milling about in
front of the Red River Saloon. Every man was armed. There were
no women on the street.

"Are we to sacrifice our brother Francisco? Are we to let him
be hung by his neck?" Padre Pilar hesitated, perhaps waiting for
Josh to answer the question. When Josh didn't, the priest simply
moved on. "For your people, Reverend, Francisco is just another Mexican, a man with no face. But the people coming to my
church know Francisco as a human being. They are knowing him

for a while now, and they are saying, one and all, that he is a gentle man by nature and could not have done this crime. So, I ask you again. Are we to sacrifice Francisco in the name of peace?"

Josh started to ask the priest how many men he was willing to sacrifice to *protect* Francisco. He didn't, yanking the words back at the last moment. "I've been giving this matter a lot of thought, Padre, as I'm sure you have. Here's what I've come to believe. Uriah Thorpe doesn't care two figs about Francisco. He wants to force the governor to call out the militia, which can't happen unless there's an actual war. Remember, if there's a battle, Mexicans against Texans, Governor Davis will have to respond. And that's the way it'll be put: Mexicans against Texans. The Texas militia, as you know, is composed only of Texans. Once called out, they won't be satisfied until they've driven Don Diego off the range."

Josh's analysis was accurate, and Padre Pilar knew it. The evidence was obvious in the resigned expression on his face, the slumped shoulders, the soft voice when he said, "There is honor, too, Reverend."

"I know that, but there's no dishonor in retreat when the forces arrayed against you are insurmountable. And you can take that from a man who's been to war. So, why not have a meeting? Don Diego and a few of the business owners, the ones who have as much to lose as Don Diego. I don't know if there's a way out of this, but we—you and me, Padre—we're obliged to prevent the bloodshed if we can. We owe it to the God we've chosen to serve."

***

Josh made his way toward the store and Sarah, who'd soon be needed again at the church. Bandages had to be changed, men to be fed, and given water. Padre Pilar had agreed to approach Don Diego, although he wasn't hopeful. For that matter, neither was Josh as he passed the Red River Saloon. There were far fewer men outside than on the night before, and they seemed, if not intimidated by Don Diego's vaqueros—they'd never admit to fear—at least cautious. The memory of last night's disaster was still fresh on their minds.

As Josh passed, a young man stepped in front of him. The boy's hair was bright orange, his face dotted with freckles. He didn't look a day over fifteen.

"Reverend, stop a minute, please. There's a friend of mine wounded last night. Name of Shane Vincent. Can you tell me how he's doin'?"

Josh didn't try to soften the blow. "Shane's dead, son. Died about two hours ago."

The boy reared back, apparently shocked. How could this have happened? Shane was only seventeen, and this boy was even younger. But that was the way of it with the young. Josh had seen it many times on the battlefield: the youngest recruits the most eager for battle yet least able to deal with the consequences.

"What's your name, son?" he asked.

"Elmer, sir. Elmer Longstreet."

"Well, you need to hear the truth, Elmer, you and all these men. Uriah Thorpe doesn't give a tinker's whit about you, no more than he did for your buddy. If you remember, Uriah stayed home last night. Now, Shane's gone and he's not comin' back, but you're still alive. You want to keep it that way, you need to get yourself to where you came from. That's what Shane wanted to do. He wanted to go home and see his momma one last time."

Josh didn't wait for a reply, noting only that the other men had listened to the message. In truth, he'd wanted to grab the boy's collar and shake some sense into him. And there was a time when he would have done just that. Not anymore, or so he told himself as he stepped into Whitegrass Mercantile to find Cole standing by the cash register, a small pile of cigarillos and a box of matches on the counter in front of him. Sarah stood behind the counter, her expression benign.

"Afternoon, Reverend," Cole said, tipping his hat, an immaculate, flat-brimmed Stetson.

"Sarah," Josh said, "let me introduce you to Mr. Cole Bradhurst. Cole . . ."

"I know exactly who he is," Sarah said. "Carmelita's already pointed him out to me."

"And how's Mr. Bradhurst been acting," Josh interrupted, "since he came into the store?"

"Respectful."

Josh locked eyes with Cole, probing for intent. The man, after all, did smoke cigarillos. But if there was no immediate threat in those blue eyes, Josh detected a steady fearlessness, along with something else. As a town marshal, Josh had looked into the eyes of men he considered born killers, only to uncover a terrifying emptiness, a vacuum, a darkness as intense as any he'd found at the bottom of a mine. That wasn't true of Cole. At bottom, he seemed vulnerable and hurt, his soul wounded by the horrors he'd witnessed. Satan had entered through that wound, ever the opportunist, as he'd entered through Josh's wounds. He'd slithered his way into Cole's soul, telling him there was no escape.

You belong to me now.

Josh followed Cole out of the store. High above, a thin layer of cloud veiled the sun, a harbinger of rain. A soaking rain, or so Josh hoped, a rain hard enough to forestall the battles to come, at least for a day.

"You seem a mite nettled, Reverend." Cole lit a cigarillo, drew the smoke into his lungs, and sighed as he exhaled. He stared at the little cigar for a moment, then said, "Times I believe these things about own me. Can't seem to go an hour without one."

Josh wasn't buying the diversion or Cole's smile. "You work for Uriah, out on the ranch?"

"Haven't seen much of the ranch these last few days, but yes, I do."

"Did you know a boy named Shane Vincent? How about Aaron Hawkins? Troy Reed? Did you know them?"

"Do you think I put guns in their hands?"

"Wouldn't know, Cole, but I'll be burying them later on if you want to attend their funerals." Josh paused for a moment, his and Cole's eyes again locked. "I've done your job. I was town marshal in Railford, New Mexico, home of the Jubilee Mining Association. Railford was a heck of a town. There were more gunslingers than miners, and a dozen professional card cheats that I let operate because they gave me a piece of their winnings."

"There a point here, Reverend?"

"Seems like there was a killing every night in Railford. Done my share, too. Fact, one time, me and my deputies caught up with three men who tried to rob the town's only bank—which the association owned, of course—in a ravine. They were boys, Cole, just like Shane and Aaron and Troy, and they were terrified. Surrender was what they had on their minds, but me and my deputies shot all three. Shot 'em down like they were no more than animals. The association bought us dinner that night. I recall thinking, at the time, that I'd crossed that line, that I couldn't be saved. I was wrong."

Josh stopped as two men approached, both stable hands. The men nodded to Josh, then entered the store. Cole turned away as the men passed, his gaze finally settling on the vaqueros outside the saddlery.

"Tell me, Reverend, for your sin, bein' part of shootin' those three boys, they didn't hang you?"

CHAPTER 27

Sarah left the store thirty minutes later, headed for the church and her patients. Josh remained behind, not in the hope of business and profit, but to host a meeting of the town's more prominent citizens. Charlie Drake, owner of the lumberyard, was first to arrive, followed closely by Pace and Mary Ellen Granger. Then Abe Jordan, the town's mute cooper, and Clemmie, his translator-wife, walked through the door. Ruddy and Smitty stepped inside fifteen minutes later, shaking the first drops of rain from their hats. Josh lost track after that, as even a few of Uriah's supporters, like the town farrier, Clancy, and the stable owner, Faro, made an appearance.

Things had gone too far, way too far. That was the general consensus. Start a war with Don Diego? The twenty vaqueros in town represented only a small fraction of the rancher's hands. Worse, any number of well-armed men could be recruited in Mexico if you had the money to pay them, seasoned veterans who'd fought in one or another of Mexico's rebellions.

To Josh's surprise, no one bought the rumor—spread by Uriah and Judah—that the Southern-Pacific had already decided to name Whitegrass as its main depot along the Pecos River. In fact, Clancy spoke for everybody when he declared, at the outset, "Won't be nothin' left of this town if there's a full-out war."

But although nobody wanted a war, nobody had a viable plan to prevent one, and Josh's report on his conversation with Padre Pilar did little to bolster confidence. "According to the padre," Josh explained, "the Mexican community is united in believing Francisco incapable of murder. These are folks who know the man personally, folks who consider him a friend. They're not about to give him up to a mob, and they may not be willing to give him up to a judge and jury. Now, Padre Pilar has promised to approach Don Diego about meeting with a small committee, but I'm pessimistic as to the outcome even should the meeting take place. We need an alternative plan."

The most obvious proposal, that a delegation be sent to Uriah, was quickly rejected. Uriah wanted the war. Judah had as much as admitted it to both Josh and Clancy.

Charlie, owner of the lumberyard, spoke up at that point. He'd been a colonel in the Civil War, commanding a brigade under Stonewall Jackson. "There won't be any action tonight," he told them. "Thorpe's too smart to send his ranch hands into battle after yesterday's slaughter. And that's even if they're willing to fight. No, if you're correct, Thorpe's already prepared for the next stage."

"And what might that be?" Pace asked.

"Men like that gunslinger, and plenty of 'em."

"Cole Bradhurst?"

"Yes, Bradhurst and his two friends, the mountain man and the dandy."

Nobody argued the point. Uriah had Don Diego's vaqueros right where he wanted them, and he'd only move when he was certain of the outcome. Not a victory, necessarily, not in Charlie's opinion. More like a standoff that guaranteed future combat and the intervention of the governor.

"We need to contact the governor ourselves," Smitty suggested.

"And tell him what?" Charlie was adamant. "Trust me, Governor Davis isn't interested in justice, or the fate of our little town. He wants to be reelected, and he won't be if he refuses to defend Texans in a fight with Mexicans. The politics of Texas aren't being run from the Pecos, boys. They're run from Dallas and Austin, from San Antonio and Houston."

Josh let the bickering continue for a good twenty minutes before he spoke up. "From what you've been saying, it appears there's only one possibility out there. We have to prevent the fight from taking place."

"And how exactly would you do that, Reverend?"

"By placing a barrier between the two sides. A human barrier." Josh looked around the room. A few appeared to know where he was going, but most seemed confused. "I'm talking about us, folks. We need to set ourselves, unarmed, in front of the jail, four at a time in shifts. I don't believe Thorpe will kill us to get to Francisco. Not because the man has a problem with murder. He won't kill unarmed town-elders because he can't justify it, to the governor or anyone else."

It seemed like everyone began to speak at the same time. The men and women assembled in the store had been considering only solutions that didn't involve personal risk. Josh was asking a lot more of them, and he hoped they'd settle on a simple truth. Without risk, there was no hope. But then the door opened and a small boy, a Mexican in a white shirt and pants, rain dripping from his sombrero, stepped inside. Surprised by the number of men standing around, it took him a moment to find his tongue.

"Señor Hill?" he finally said.

"Yes?"

"The Padre says you should come now."

***

Don Diego proved to be quite ordinary in appearance, a short man in a black suit with a cutaway jacket and black boots suitable to the trail. His white shirt was buttoned to the throat and he wore no tie, as was the custom. His features and expression, by contrast, were anything but ordinary. The man wore his dignity like a coat of arms, his chin raised, his mouth defiantly firm. His eyes were dark and fierce, as were the eyes of the three men who'd accompanied him. These men were dressed in black shirts and trousers, like the man who'd led the vaqueros into Whitegrass.

Although Don Diego shook hands with Josh, Pace, and Doc, the three townsmen who'd come to the meeting, his companions stood off to the rear, hands always near the pistols jammed behind their belts. The two sides were meeting in a small room at the back of the mission. Padre, of course, would never allow weapons into the church proper.

Doc spoke first. He'd been chosen primarily because he'd treated men and women from Don Diego's ranch in the past. As he was the only doctor within a hundred miles, they'd had no choice in the matter.

"Don Diego," he began, "I hope I'm not bein' too forward when I say that we're acquainted, you and me."

"You are not." Don Diego spoke barely accented English. Rumor had it that he'd been educated back East. "And I thank you, Doctor, for the care you showed my daughter. Her leg has fully healed, and she walks with only a slight limp. I was thinking for a time that she might be crippled."

"Excellent." Cassidy took a step forward, his demeanor, in its own way, as assertive as Don Diego's. "I don't believe I'm mistaken, either, when I say that you know me as a man of my word. Correct me if I'm bein' too presumptuous."

Don Diego's mouth widened slightly. He was probably amused, Josh decided, because Doc had forced a response the rancher would prefer not to make.

"You are not, Doctor."

"And these men with me, I've known them for a long time, and I tell you that they are also men of their word." Doc paused, but Don Diego failed to react. "We speak for the tradesmen in Whitegrass. We don't want a war."

"This is up to Señor Thorpe. We will make no trouble for the town if the jail is not again attacked."

"It's Thorpe who wants a fight, as you know. That's his set course, and he won't be deterred by the likes of us." Doc gestured to his companions. "But I'll let Reverend Hill speak for us now, if you don't mind. I'm sure Padre's already mentioned him."

When Don Diego nodded, Josh stepped forward and began to speak. He kept his language simple but his message blunt, so there'd be no confusing the issue.

"I'll start by speaking for myself, Don Diego, and not for the committee. I don't believe Francisco murdered Elijah Norton. I believe that Elijah was attacked by a man named Cole Bradhurst, a gunman who works for Uriah Thorpe."

"How do you know this?"

"First, because Bradhurst showed up at the ranch shortly after the attack, so he was in the vicinity and he could have done it. Second, because he came close to admitting it only two hours ago."

"The man, Bradhurst, he had no dispute with Señor Norton?"

"None."

"In this case, the killing must have been ordered by Thorpe. That is what you are saying?" Don Diego waited until Josh nodded, then added, "But why does Thorpe wish to murder Elijah Norton?"

"Because the only safe ford of the Pecos River is located on the Norton farm, and Thorpe's had his eye on the crossing for a long time. He's made offers to buy the farm in the past, and he made another to Rachel Norton the day after she buried her husband. The message . . . Well, let's say that Mr. Thorpe's a man accustomed to getting what he wants. But that's not really the point here. No, the point is that Thorpe never expected Francisco to be arrested and has no real interest in Francisco's fate. What he did know, sir, was that you'd react to a lynch mob coming after Francisco and the simple fact, though you may find it unpleasant, is that you've given him exactly what he wants. That's because you're a man of honor up against a man without honor. If you fight Thorpe, you'll lose, but you have to fight him to preserve your dignity. You have to fight him to save face."

Don Diego's reaction was minimal. His nostrils flared and he shifted his weight to his heels. Josh only noticed because he was expecting Don Diego to be offended. The rancher was being called a fool, a sucker, and he didn't like it.

"Forgive me," Josh continued, "for speaking so directly. But there's no time for diplomacy. The powder's been packed and the fuse lit. Your men, where they're positioned at Pablo Sierra's saddlery, are inviting an attack, not preventing one. This is exactly what Thorpe wants."

"And I am to do what, Señor? Retreat and allow Francisco to be . . . to be lynched? This is the word you *anglos* use, yes? Lynched?"

"Thorpe's not interested in Francisco. He's interested in you. If you order your men back to the ranch and let the town protect Francisco, Thorpe will almost certainly withdraw. He's already lost fourteen cowboys—three dead and eleven injured. He won't sacrifice more of his men, not with a ranch to run. And there's little point to hiring professionals if there's no one for them to fight. You can prevent this war. It lies within your power."

Josh didn't demand a response. It was too early for that. Instead, he stepped back and allowed Pace, Francisco's lawyer, to speak. Well prepared, Pace opened his mouth, but his words were cut short by a pair of gunshots that came, not from the direction of the saddlery or the jail, but from the other end of town.

Josh was first through the door, Don Diego forgotten, but it took him a minute to dash from behind the church to the street. By then, men were running past the hardware store and the stables, past the Red River Saloon and the Bright Chance Hotel, directly to the Whitegrass Mercantile. Though he remained frozen, as if his boots were nailed to the wooden boardwalk, Josh's first thought was that Sarah, at least, was safe. Still occupied with her patients, she'd yet to come home when he left for the church. The store and house were empty.

"Reverend, Reverend?" Gentle in tone, the voice belonged to Doc, who laid a hand on Josh's shoulder. "Let's get up there, Reverend."

"No, it's all right. Sarah is at the church."

But then the impossible happened. Sarah stepped through the doorway and onto the boardwalk. There was blood on her arms and dress, bright red blood, running blood, visible even at this distance. Josh felt, for a moment, as though he'd take the only escape available and pass out. Something in his heart seemed to burst, as though the blood flowing from his wife was his own, and his first steps when Doc urged him forward were stumbling, the gait of a drunk afraid to go home.

CHAPTER 28

Cole entered his boss's great room for the second time since his arrival. Uriah was standing before the room's enormous hearth, poking at the ashes of a long-dead fire. The pose, so obviously theatrical, disgusted Cole, and he found himself wondering what he'd uncover if he dug down to the root of Uriah's being, the root of his soul, the root of his heart. If anything.

And his own soul, his own heart?

Cole put the question to one side as he crossed the room, passing his boss's stuffed wolves, stepping over the skin of the trophy rattlesnake.

"You wanted to see me?"

Uriah straightened as he turned to face his gunman. "What do you think? Will they be reliable?"

Uriah was referring to the twenty men assembled in the largest of the ranch's barns. They claimed to be seasoned warriors, veterans who'd never stopped fighting. From the range wars to the north, to security work at the mines in Nevada and Arizona, to law enforcement jobs in the cotton towns of East Texas, violence was at the heart of the way they earned a living. Yet they were not undisciplined outlaws or baby-faced cowboys. They were hard and serious men. The only question was whether Cole, a man they didn't know, could exact enough respect to convert them into an effective fighting force.

"I believe they'll do," Cole said, which was the only thing his boss wanted to hear. "But all this preparation, it must be for a reason, which you've been keepin' to yourself. Now I got to know, boss. What is it you want to happen tomorrow night?"

Uriah bristled, sensing an underlying insolence. Ordinarily, he'd bring his employee down to earth, but he was so close now, close to realizing a goal he'd set for himself on the day he crossed the Pecos River. He would have the biggest ranch in Texas, even bigger than the King Ranch. He would have all of Texas west of the Pecos and east of the Rio Grande. Quickly, almost breathlessly, he spelled out his plans for the following night. Only when he finished did he rediscover his ordinary voice.

"We're almost there, Cole," he said. "Almost there."

Uriah walked to an elaborately carved chest, Spanish by the look of it. He lifted the lid, removed a bottle of brandy, and poured a single drink. "The negotiations are over. All we need do is seal the deal."

Annabelle Thorpe chose that moment to make an appearance. Wearing a midnight-green dress that clung to her torso and hips, she didn't merely walk across the room. The undulation of her hips and shoulders were too pronounced for that.

"Good evening, Mr. Bradhurst," she said as she passed.

Cole watched her pour herself a drink, endure Uriah's frown, slowly spin to again face Cole.

"Cheers," she said.

Cole smiled and raised his glass, knowing he could kill Uriah right now, kill Uriah and take his wife. She wouldn't resist, would most likely welcome both the demise of her husband and the pleasure that comes of being with a man who didn't treat her as a possession.

"Don't you have work to do, Cole?" Uriah said.

Cole felt the nerve endings in his fingertips twitch. For a brief moment, as Shane Vincent's image danced before his eyes, he almost lost control. Then he suddenly turned and left the room. Cole had been a good soldier throughout the war, fighting on when others deserted the cause. He hadn't liked many of his superiors and almost hated Jeff Davis, who'd sacrificed thousands upon thousands after all hope of victory was lost. Still, Cole had served on, as he'd pledged to do, a helpless witness to a pointless slaughter. Toward the end, boys of fifteen and sixteen years were rushed to the front. And like Shane, they rarely survived their first battle.

Cole found Irish Jack Kelly standing outside the barn where the rest of his troops awaited. The cowboys at the ranch had taken to calling him the Dandy. The name fit him perfectly. Today Irish Jack wore a double-breasted vest, royal blue with a red brocade. His black trousers held a knife-edge crease and his cravat, worn over a snow-white shirt with ruffled sleeves, matched the vest.

"Evenin', Cole."

Bradhurst looked the man over for a moment. Irish Jack disliked and mistrusted Uriah as much as Cole did. Did he also mistrust Cole?

"Inside," he told the gunman, "I'm gonna need you to back my play."

"You expectin' trouble?"

"Could be, Jack."

Irish Jack stared at Cole, probably in the hope Cole would supply a few more details. When he didn't, Irish Jack merely nodded before loosening the Colt in its holster.

"I'm with ya, boss."

Cole reached for the door handle, then stopped as his eye caught movement off in the distance. For a long moment, he watched a narrow tunnel, a funnel cloud, move across the scrub, touching down, bouncing up, touching down again. Cole had witnessed much larger storms in Nebraska and Oklahoma, but the tornados here, though short-lived, were said to be equally intense.

"Let's go, Jack."

Cole stepped into the barn, bringing all conversation to a halt. The twenty men inside were, indeed, men, not boys out for an adventure. They knew there'd soon be a fight. Only the details were lacking, the nature of the risk. Naturally, they riveted their attention on the man with the answers when he made an appearance, in this slight way acknowledging Cole's authority.

For his part, Cole came all the way inside the barn before focusing on his woodsman, George Thompson. Word had come back to the ranch an hour before. Someone had fired into Reverend Hill's store, wounding the preacher's wife. Cole was sure he'd be blamed, though he had spent the entire afternoon at the ranch. The same could not be said of George. Another of Uriah's betrayals.

"George," Cole said, "last night, against my instructions, you took a bottle of whiskey into combat. Do you deny it?"

"Can't see how it's your business, long as I done what I was told." George glanced down at the Army Colt tucked inside his buckskin jacket, then back at Cole before repeating himself. "Can't see how it's any of your business."

Cole's right hand was already by his side. If it came to a fight, and Cole sincerely hoped it would, Thompson's single-action Army Colt would be no match for the lighter Schofield revolver in Cole's holster. That would be true even if the man was entirely sober, which he obviously was not.

"You're fired, Thompson. Pack your stuff, get going, and keep going."

George Thompson lumbered to his feet, his age and weight, not to mention the alcohol he'd been consuming ever since he woke up in the morning, slowing him down. Cole wondered if the alcohol had also made him stupid enough to allow Cole to kill him. The preacher's wife—he couldn't quite remember her name—was a good woman, an innocent. There could be no justifying . . .

Suddenly, Cole recalled Uriah's first orders. He was to murder Elijah Norton *and* his wife, to remove any impediment to Uriah's acquiring the farm.

"What if I like it where I am?" George said. "What if I decide to stay? What then, boy?"

"Then I'm going to kill you, George. Right here and right now."

The silence that followed was profound. Every eye was riveted to the scene, and these veterans all knew that Cole wasn't bluffing, as they knew the lesson was meant for each of them. Cole was in charge. He would give orders, and they would take them. That was how you survived battles, a chain of command that exacted the strictest discipline. Every other approach resulted in something more like a bar fight than a battle.

Cole watched George's face redden as the truth set in. The mountain man had spent his whole life confronting obstacles, never turning away from a fight, always charging forward. That would no longer work, and he knew it. Time had caught up with him. He was too old, too slow. If he wanted to live, he'd have to turn tail, maybe run over to the house and whine to Uriah. Still, his hand moved, almost of itself, in tiny jerks toward the pistol in his belt.

Cole calmly responded, his own fingers dropping below the grips of his weapon. His eyes, too, remained calm, and it was obvious to every gunman in the room, including George, that Cole was only waiting for an excuse.

George finally broke, his will vanishing in an instant as he brought his hands together, interlacing his fingers. He wanted to say something but couldn't find the words. That wasn't true of Cole.

"George, I'm giving you an hour to leave the ranch. And don't think you can appeal to Mr. Thorpe. If you're still on the ranch an hour from now, I'll kill you. And that goes for the rest of you men. If you should see George an hour from now, kill him and I'll see you're rewarded. Goodbye, George."

Twenty minutes later, with George gone, Cole had the full attention of the remaining gunmen, including Irish Jack, who was all smiles. In asking for Irish Jack's help, Cole had more or less promoted him to second in command.

"That man never saw a bar of soap in his life," Irish Jack said. "He stunk worse than the buffalo he skinned." Irish Jack tucked his thumbs beneath the lapels of his vest. "I was embarrassed to be seen with him. The slob was ruinin' my reputation with the ladies."

Cole allowed the little joke but then got down to business. First, he used heaps of straw to build a replica of the town, naming the various businesses, locating the jail, the saddle-maker's shop, and the Red River Saloon. When he was sure his men had the basics down, he rose to his feet and laid out the plan of battle.

"The enemy—the men you're to kill and the men who will try to kill you—will be at two locations. The sheriff and one other man will be positioned in front of the jail. Five additional deputies will be stationed on the roof." Cole pointed to the heap of straw representing the jail. "Don Diego's men, vaqueros and not fighting men, will be over here." He pointed to the heap representing the saddlery. "Some will be in front, others inside or out back. Altogether, you'll be facing off against twenty vaqueros. Any questions?"

One man spoke up, a middle-aged man named Deuce Coleman. Deuce had the practical look of a man who'd survived many a conflict and expected to survive this one.

"The jail and the saddle-maker's shop, are they made of wood?"

"Afraid not, Deuce. The jail's of brick and the saddlery's of thick stucco. You can't shoot through the walls. But I'll get to that part later." Cole took a second to organize his thoughts. Some part of his mind couldn't stop thinking about Sarah Hill, wondering whether or not she was alive. The wooden walls of the Whitegrass Mercantile hadn't stopped the bullet that struck her, had barely slowed it down.

"We'll start drifting into town right after sun up, one or two at a time, and go directly to the Red River Saloon. We won't need rifles. They'll be supplied later on—new Winchesters. The main thing is to get out of sight and stay out of sight until we're ready to move. If we choose our own time and fight as a unit, we can minimize casualties."

Cole glanced at the men, several of whom were nodding their heads. So far, so good. "Now, we'll be inside the Red River by noon and it'll be nightfall before we move out, so you're gonna find yourself with time on your hands. Personally, I don't mind if you consort with some of the ladies in the saloon, as long as you don't drink, not a one of you." Cole was expecting some sort of protest, but there was none. "Come nightfall, you'll be divided in half. Ten of you will walk—walk, not run—along the board-walk until you reach the feed store. There'll be sacks of grain and a half-loaded wagon outside. That'll be your cover when you engage the vaqueros. The second group will be stationed on the saloon's roof. I'm going to divide this group in half—five to back the play of the men on the ground, and five to engage the sheriff and his deputies. The Red River Saloon is two stories high, while the jail and saddlery are one story, so you'll have the high ground. Any questions so far?"

The man who spoke up was the youngest in the group. His name was Terry Sedgewick, and he claimed to have been a drum-mer boy in A. P. Hill's brigade. "All this fightin'? I ain't got a problem with it. Only thing, Cole, I'd like to know what we're tryin' to accomplish. If we have to charge either one of these buildings, they'll be the devil to pay."

"I was just gettin' to that, Terry. First, the sheriff will most likely be sitting outside the jail. You're not to kill him. You're to let him retreat into the jail. Mr. Thorpe wants him safe, him and his prisoner."

Cole paused to let the message hit home. Uriah wanted blood-shed—vaquero blood and Texan blood. But as he'd carefully ex-plained, there was nothing to win, even should every vaquero be killed. The battle tomorrow night would be no more than a skir-mish, an opening act. Leaving Francisco alive, with the sheriff to protect him, would force Don Diego to divide his forces between the town and his ranch, much to Uriah's advantage.

"What about the men on the roof of the jail?"

"Considerin' the obvious, that they'll be tryin' their best to kill us, I think it's only fair that we return the favor. But it won't matter all that much because this fight's only going to last a few minutes. You'll hear me fire my pistol three times, rapid fire, when I'm ready to break off. At that point, the men on the street, including me, will retreat to the Red River, while the men on the roof will provide cover fire until we're inside, then come down. Our horses will be saddled and ready behind the saloon. We're to mount up immediately, ride back to the ranch, and establish a perimeter around Mr. Thorpe's home. Just in case Don Diego comes callin'."

There was more to be sorted out, but they had all night if necessary. The most important goal had already been accomplished. As Cole went along, the men had nodded, accepting his authority, at least for the length of this first encounter. His commitment to be among the men on the boardwalk, though mentioned casually, had gotten the biggest reaction. They would all, Cole included, take the same risks.

"All right, boys, I think we understand each other. This plan comes directly from Mr. Thorpe. Our job is to pull it off with minimal casualties. Now, if you go outside, you'll find two cases of good whiskey sittin' against the side of the barn. That'll get you started, and I'll have grub sent in later on. Enjoy tonight. Tomorrow morning, we ride. Tomorrow night, we fight." Cole waited until the men nodded agreement, their expressions grim as befitted the task they'd been assigned. Then he said, "One more thing. Mr. Thorpe will join us in town, but not in the operation. Your orders will come from me. Mr. Thorpe is only there to enjoy the show."

CHAPTER 29

For the first hour after a bullet found his wife's shoulder, Josh Hill almost came to believe that he was asleep and dreaming. The world around him, as Doc led him along the boardwalk to Whitegrass Mercantile, became suddenly veiled, as though Josh were looking at the town through a curtain. At one point, he even wiped at his eyes, but the illusion would not fade. His mind worked no better. It kept repeating the same sentence: Sarah is at the church, at the church, at the church, at the church. Never mind the porcelain-white face, the closed eyes, the bright blood flowing from her shoulder and down her arm fast enough to drip from her fingers. Josh barely noticed when Pace lifted Sarah into his arms and ran with her toward Doc's office, barely noticed the doctor following, moving fast despite his limp. Josh, his expression that of a bewildered steer trying to make sense of a slaughterhouse, didn't move, not an inch.

"Reverend? Reverend Hill?"

So faint that Josh initially failed to recognize his own name or the name of the speaker, the words seemed to come from a great distance. But then a hand dropped to his shoulder and shook him hard.

"Reverend, you've got to move."

Josh finally recognized the voice. Mary Ellen Granger was literally pushing him toward the doctor's office. Josh resisted momentarily, his brain still refusing to accept what his eyes had seen. He looked at Mary Ellen as though she had an answer to some question he'd forgotten to ask. Then he nodded and began to walk, slowly at first, then faster and faster, until by the time he reached the doctor's office, he was finally running.

He was still running as he came inside and heard his wife scream for the first time. Through an open door, he saw Doc at work. He'd cut the dress from Sarah's left shoulder, exposing the mangled flesh, the protruding bone. Now he was fishing for the bullet, sliding forceps into the entry wound, probing, probing. Josh had seen it all during the war. He knew the bullet had to come out before the bleeding was addressed. And addressed it would be. Martha Robinson was already building a fire in a small stove. A flat piece of iron lay atop the stove. The iron would be red-hot before it was brought into play.

"For God's sake," Josh said, "give her something for the pain, please Doc."

Doc looked up but said nothing, only nodding at Martha Robinson, who closed the door to his surgery.

Josh Hill was a man of God. He was supposed to drop to his knees and beg a merciful God to spare his wife, to make her whole, and he knew it. But his mind wouldn't remain still, thoughts flying back and forth like ricocheting bullets, and he could only remember snatches of the prayers and Bible passages he'd fought so hard to memorize. Passages that now seemed to mock his most cherished beliefs.

Blessed are the peacemakers?

Blessed are the meek?

Blessed are the pure in heart?

They're blessed, all right, some part of him told some other part that didn't want to hear. Blessed with a bullet.

Josh had seen the bodies piled up in Atlanta, the bodies of children, of women, of the old and infirm. And Sarah? That arm would never work again, not as it was supposed to. And that's assuming she didn't lose the arm. Or die, taking her unborn child with her.

Sarah screamed again, then again, then began to sob. Every sound tore at Josh's heart, and when he finally summoned the courage to pray, only a single word, repeated over and over again, issued from his mouth.

Please, please, please . . .

Josh was still mumbling when Pace walked into the office, his face so red and tense that he seemed to be holding his breath. "The shot came from out on the prairie somewhere. No sign of the bushwhacker."

The words seemed little more than gibberish to Josh. This was the work of one man, the product of one man's ambitions, just as the lost war, the lost cause, was the product of a few scheming planters who managed to spook the herd. Why did God allow men like this to control events? Men lost to the effects of their aspirations? Why would God allow a man like Cole to murder a man like Elijah? The questions were as old as Cain and Abel, as was the answer: God's will is beyond question.

An answer that was, at that moment, no answer at all.

"You think I don't know who's responsible?" he asked Pace. "You think I need proof?"

"Reverend, please." This time it was Mary Ellen Granger, who stood to his left. "It's time for prayer now. You must pray for your wife."

From inside the surgery, Sarah's screams had faded to a continuous moan, an awful keening sound made all the worse for Josh knowing the cause. Sarah's strength was fading. Though her pain had not diminished, she could no longer summon the energy to scream.

As though someone or something had opened a door he didn't know existed, a series of thoughts stole into Josh's mind. Uriah had done this. Uriah and Uriah alone. Eliminate Uriah and the violence will end because there's nobody to take his place. Eliminate Uriah and the violence will end.

The conclusion seemed to release him, as though he'd accomplished some necessary task. He finally allowed himself to sit, to think, and to pray.

Love for your enemies ran through the Gospels. "*Beloved, let us love one another, for love is from God; and everyone who loves is born of God and knows God.*" That was John, but Josh might have quoted any number of verses. And he needn't have stopped with the Gospels, either. From Exodus to Isaiah and Job, the message was everywhere. Love brings you closer to God. Hate pulls you away.

You made us weak, Josh said to himself. You made us so weak, and You seeded your creation with loathsome beasts like Uriah Thorpe, beasts who arouse the very parts of ourselves we're charged with rejecting. But now I ask only for the strength to see my wife through her injuries, to hold her once again, to cherish her as I've cherished her from the day we met. This is a woman who's served You always. Even as a child she served You. Please, You who are all-powerful, reach out to touch her spirit, to keep her alive, soul and body. Long ago, when I lay close to death, she came to me in the evening, seeming one of Your angels, and placed a Bible in my hand. I believe you're in need of this. That's what she said . . ."

The door to the surgery opened at that moment and Doc stepped out. Behind him, Josh saw his wife lying on a long, narrow table, unmoving.

"She's asleep, Reverend," Cassidy said. "C'mon outside."

The two men stepped into a cool, gentle mist that would soon become a steady rain. The boardwalk was deserted on their side, even before the Red River Saloon. Across the way, three vaqueros squatted with their backs against the wall of the saddlery, bodies draped in ponchos, sombreros pulled down almost to their eyes.

"We got the bullet out and stopped the bleeding," Doc said. "Mostly thanks to Martha."

"And Sarah?"

"I've given her laudanum and she's asleep. Look, I'm not generally in the business of predicting, but I'll go out on a limb this time. Barring infection, I believe Sarah will pull through."

"And her arm?"

"She'll keep it, again barring infection."

"C'mon, Doc. I was there, remember."

Doc nodded once. "The bullet took her high on her left shoulder, shattering the clavicle and the humerus. But there's likely no damage to the nerves that control the arm. Sarah was able to make a fist and fold her elbow. In the end, her shoulder will be stiff, possibly frozen, but she'll be able to use her arm and her hand."

"Thanks for bein' honest, Doc," Josh said.

"Don't thank me yet, Reverend." Doc lit his cigar and drew down the smoke. "Look, there's no good way to put this, so I'll say it plain. The shock, the blood loss, the pain, they were all too much for her. Sarah lost her baby."

CHAPTER 30

At Josh's insistence, Sarah was taken from the surgery back to her home instead of the makeshift hospital at the church. Some doctors believed that infections could somehow be transferred from one patient to another. How? Nobody knew, but Josh wasn't taking any chances. Better she should be home anyway, in her own house, in her own bed. Although never a medic, he would care for her himself if necessary.

It wasn't necessary, as it turned out. Shortly after sundown, he answered a knock on the door to find Carmelita standing on the other side. She barely nodded before marching past him and into the bedroom he shared with Sarah. To his surprise, she lowered her face to the heaped bandages on Sarah's shoulder, then drew a long breath through her nose.

"These," she said, pointing to a stack of coiled bandages on the bureau, "need to be boiled. If you will please to make the stove on fire, I will see to it."

Josh stared at this intruder for a moment, knowing she'd been sent by Rachel, who could ill afford to lose her with a crop to harvest.

"All right," he said, but as he turned, he felt something drop away, some part of himself held in check by pure necessity. Sarah had needed his care, and that overrode any personal feelings. Now he felt a shift toward the man he'd once been, quick to anger and suffering no disrespect from anyone. He tried to catch himself, to slow the descent, going so far as to tell himself that he was becoming Cole Bradhurst, one of the men he held responsible for

Sarah's terrible injury. But there seemed no stopping the emotions that boiled up.

Josh scooped up the bandages and carried them into the kitchen. He built a fire in the cooking stove from kindling Sarah had collected, then filled a stockpot with water, set it atop the stove, and placed the bandages inside. Would boiling have any effect on Sarah's recovery? Josh didn't know and didn't care to speculate. His mind was on other things. That was true even when he looked in on his still-sleeping wife.

"I've set water to boiling," he told Carmelita.

"Good." Carmelita reached toward Sarah's damaged arm. "I am going to remove these dirty bandages now. They are not helping. Please, leave me to this job."

Josh had a few minutes until the water began to boil. He took advantage of the time by running down to a storeroom on the first floor. There, behind a crate of porcelain teapots, he found a long case that he'd carried throughout the war and afterward, even on his last trek through the mountains.

For a few seconds before raising the lid, Josh hesitated, as though opening a door through which anything might enter. But then, his jaw tightening, he flipped the lid up to reveal a Whitworth sniper rifle with its telescopic sight still attached.

The Yankees had equipped their snipers, whenever possible, with breechloading Sharps rifles. These were unavailable to the Rebels, as were the Enfields and Springfields also commonly used by the Union. The South had been forced to rely on the Whitworth, manufactured in England. The Whitworth was an odd duck, with its hexagonal bore, and Josh had been skeptical the first time he handled one. But the rifle had proved itself when it counted. In the field, Josh had been able to hit targets with deadly accuracy out to a distance of six hundred yards. And even at eight hundred yards, his hit rate was north of 50 percent.

Josh put the stock to his shoulder. Cut off the snake's head, he told himself, and the body will die. With no one to pay them, mercenaries stop fighting. Josh laughed to himself. He hadn't been paid, not one Confederate dollar, for the final two years of the war. But he'd been fighting for a cause, the money irrelevant. Now . . .

"Reverend?" The voice at the head of the stairs belonged to Carmelita. "Señora Hill asks for you."

Josh was at his wife's side within seconds, trying not to look at her uncovered wound, at the torn and mangled flesh as he took her right hand in his. He was a man of words, a preacher, yet he could find no adequate words for what lay ahead.

"Sarah," he finally muttered, "I'm sorry. I'm so, so sorry."

"The baby?" Sarah squeezed his hand, her grip so faint he barely felt the pressure. "Is the baby all right?"

Josh considered lying. Just get her through these first few days, he told himself. Tell her when she's strong enough to bear the truth. Instead, the words tumbled from his mouth.

"Gone," he said. "Our baby is gone."

The cry that rose from Sarah's chest ripped through Josh's body, through his mind, through his soul. It brought Carmelita into the room. Josh watched, his mouth open, as Carmelita gave Sarah a dose of laudanum provided by Doc, as Sarah's cries slowly died away, as her eyes finally closed and she finally slept. Only then did he allow himself to feel the only emotion possible under the circumstances. He raged.

***

Later that night, in the early hours of the new day, with Carmelita and Sarah asleep, with the town of Whitegrass asleep, with even the Red River Saloon closed, Josh left the store through the back. He walked straight out onto the prairie for several hundred yards, then circled the town, pushing through a light rain, the Whitworth wrapped in oilcloth tucked beneath his arm. In no hurry, he traced a wide semicircle, searching for the right spot.

Josh had spent three years finding right spots, three years putting individual men within the Whitworth's sight, three years gently compressing the trigger, three years watching men die. He never fired into a crowd. His bullets were never one of thousands flying back and forth across the battlefield. His bullets killed human beings, men with faces, with hopes and fears, with friends and families, but with no futures. In less than a second, he took everything they had or ever would have.

Josh found his nest to the south of his little church, four hundred yards out on the prairie. Two patches of prickly pear cactus were separated by a flat boulder that rose about six inches above the soil. The nest offered a clear view of main street and the front of every building on its north side, including the Red River Saloon. It offered perfect cover as well. From this distance, surrounded by cactus, from a prone position with the Whitworth's barrel steadied on the rock, he'd be all but invisible. He'd be all but invisible, and he wouldn't miss.

CHAPTER 31

Josh made his way back to his home, still unseen, after wrapping the Whitworth rifle in oilcloth and hiding it inside the stand of prickly pear. He managed to get a couple of hours of fitful sleep, lying on a sheepskin rug spread across the floor, but then Carmelita woke him shortly after sunrise.

"Your wife calls for you," she said before she crossed the room and busied herself at the wood stove. "She is in great pain, Reverend."

"Have you given her another dose of the laudanum?"

"She wants her mind to be . . . to be clear when she speaks. I will give this to her afterward."

Josh would have liked to wash up, but he went at once to Sarah's side, steeling himself as he found a chair next to the bed, sat down, and took her hand. He was relieved to find Sarah's shoulder bandaged, the bandages clean and not discolored or tinged with blood. Nevertheless, as he leaned forward to kiss her lips, gently, Josh felt tears start behind his eyes.

"I love you so much, my darling. I'm so, so sorry."

Sarah shook her head, still so weak the gesture took seconds to complete. "How?" she asked.

"How did it happen?"

"Yes."

"Two shots through the store's wall. I think they were fired randomly, without a clear target. I think they were supposed to send a message."

"Well, they certainly did that."

Sarah had made a joke, despite everything, and Josh marveled at her strength. "The shooter wasn't caught, Sarah, but I have to think it was Cole. He threatened me earlier in the day."

A brief silence followed as Sarah put her thoughts together. Finally, she said, pausing after every few words, "Threatening you doesn't . . . make him guilty, Josh . . . Any more than Francisco being found with Elijah . . . makes Francisco guilty. But I called you in because . . . because I want the truth. My shoulder. How bad is it?"

Josh didn't consider lying because he knew she'd never forgive him if he did. The trust that held their marriage together would be lost. Josh squeezed his wife's hand before speaking.

"Doc says you'll probably be able to bend your elbow and use your hands, but your shoulder will be stiff, maybe frozen."

Sarah looked up at the ceiling as a tear rolled along her cheek. Then she began to sob. Josh wanted to pick her up, to cradle her in his arms, but that was impossible, and he could only wait, stroking the side of her face, kissing her forehead, until she calmed.

"Josh," she finally said, the words seeming to come from somewhere beyond her lungs, "we can make another baby, right? Tell me, please."

"We can make a dozen, Sarah. We can have tribes of babies. Herds, if you like. Whole civilizations."

Josh stayed for another ten minutes, offering whatever comfort he could, until the pain threatened to overwhelm his wife. Then he called in Carmelita, who gave Sarah a dose of the pain medicine. A few minutes later, Sarah was asleep, her expression peaceful.

In the kitchen, Josh found two bowls filled with porridge made from ground oats. A platter in the center of the table held four buttered biscuits. A bottle held milk fresh from the O'Maras' small herd. Suddenly famished, Josh sat down and began to eat. Carmelita joined him a moment later. Josh wasn't fooled, though neither spoke for a time. The young woman on the far side of the table had quick, dark eyes that probed relentlessly. Carmelita had something to say and she intended to say it. She wouldn't ask for permission.

"My parents were Tejanos in the revolution," she finally declared. "You know what this is, Reverend."

"I do."

In the Texas war for independence, a good portion of the Spanish-speaking population fought with the Texans. Calling themselves Tejanos, they believed they'd get a better deal from the Americans than they ever got from Santa Ana and his fellow aristocrats in Mexico City.

"I have a father, Manuel, and a brother, Rafael," Carmelita continued. "Both are riding with Sam Houston. They fight many battles until at last battle of San Jacinto, Rafael is killed. Texas is then free, yes? And we are all one, yes, all brothers? So why is this that Texans come one night to steal my father's farm, so many that we cannot fight?" Carmelita paused long enough to sigh, but she wasn't finished. "We are forced to flee, but we cannot go to Mexico because we have fought for Texas. So, we go north with no money, with nothing, and my father falls ill. *Dysenteria*. If he has proper food, if he has rest, then maybe he lives. But he has nothing, Reverend, and he dies by the side of the road without even a roof above his head. My mother follows soon after, from what except grief I do not know. I know only that I was fifteen years and on my own."

Josh raised his hands. He didn't know where Carmelita was going, but he found himself resisting her steady tone. "Why are you telling me this?" he finally asked.

"Because you are not praying, Reverend. Because I am looking into your heart and seeing the darkness. Because I have been holding this story in my own heart for a too long time."

"All right, then." There was nothing else for Josh to say to this woman who cared for his wife. Carmelita's devotion, after even one night, was obvious.

"Every place I go, I am used, as if I am not a person, as if I am a toy for men to play with, until I am hating everyone and everything. I am hating the ants I step on. I am hating the worms I dig out of ground when I try to fish. I am hating the man who takes my fish away from me. I am most of all hating the men who buy my time in the Red River. I think I will never stop this hating. I think I will die hating. I am thinking hell cannot be worse than the life I am already leading. Then I hear about you from another of the women, and what is left of my soul carries me to your church and you show me another way. You teach that if the Lord can forgive me, I can also forgive the world. This you must also do, Reverend. I can see the darkness that reaches out to you, because I have lived in it. You cannot escape by hating. You must pray."

CHAPTER 32

Josh witnessed the arrival of the first pair of Uriah's soldiers from the boardwalk in front of the store not long after breakfast. They walked their horses in from the west, not from the east and the Pecos, which caught his attention. What's more, they carried pistols, but not rifles, which also put Josh on guard. Pistols were town weapons and poorly suited to the empty scrublands where the Comanche and Apache still reigned.

Stone-faced, looking neither right nor left, the men carried Josh right back to his days as Railford's town marshal. When men like these rode into town, Josh had alerted his deputies without delay. Then, as often as not employing the element of surprise, he'd put them, unarmed, on the next train out of Railford. Now he watched the pair tie up their horses and enter the Red River Saloon.

"Mornin', Reverend."

Josh turned to find Clemmie Jordan holding a cast-iron stew pot with a towel wrapped around the handle. Her husband Abe stood just behind her.

"Cooked this up for you this morning," she said as she handed the pot to Josh. "You know, Reverend, we're heartbroken, the whole town. Sarah was the best of . . ."

"Not 'was', Clemmie," Josh said. "Just now, Sarah is asleep and comfortable. No sign of fever. She's being tended by Carmelita Mendoza."

"Carmelita." Clemmie shook her head. "That girl has turned out to be a wonder. First Rachel, now Sarah; the girl never asks for nothin'. Reverend, when you convert 'em, you really convert 'em."

Over Abe's shoulder, Josh watched a man walk his horse along main street, a stranger armed only with a handgun. Like the first pair, he tied his horse in front of the Red River Saloon, then strolled inside.

***

Josh would have liked nothing better than to be left to himself and his wife, but it was not to be. By midmorning, he'd piled up enough food in his kitchen, gifts from his neighbors, to feed the garrison at Fort Baxter. The talk began, in each case, with word of Sarah's condition, but then turned to the vaqueros still positioned before the saddlery, the cowboys inside the Red River Saloon and Uriah's ambitions.

How to stop Uriah? Don Diego was their only hope, so they said, but that hope was dashed before noon when Pace, Josh, and Doc were called to the mission. Don Diego was not in attendance, and the message he delivered through the padre was depressingly simple. Don Diego's vaqueros would remain where they were. And while they would not start a war, they were prepared to fight one if attacked or if an attempt was made to storm the jail. That left the final decision in Uriah's hands.

"Don Diego," Padre Pilar told them, "he says a war with Thorpe, it has to be happening, sooner or later. Don Diego is not a fool, *señores*. He knows this governor will act. But Don Diego's ancestors are coming here when America is still a colony of the English. He will not be driven out. If he must die, he will die on his own land."

Josh left believing that Don Diego and Uriah had one thing in common. Neither gave a whit about Whitegrass or its residents. They were playing a bigger game, at least in their own minds. Uriah saw his chance, and he was taking it. Don Diego knew that more and more Americans were flooding into Texas every day, as they had been since the end of the Civil War that left the South destitute. The rancher had nothing to gain by waiting.

In the meantime, Uriah's fighters continued to arrive, singly and in pairs, throughout the morning. Josh counted twelve but had to assume there were others he'd missed. Unless he stopped it, the range war would begin tonight.

Only a few minutes later, Uriah, accompanied by Cole, rode into town. Josh stood with the sheriff in front of the jail as they cantered by.

"You see what I see?" Josh asked.

"Sure do, Reverend."

"Have you seen the men who've been arriving all morning?"

"Seen them too."

"These ain't cowboys, Trey."

"Now look here, Reverend, this whole business ain't of my makin', but I got to deal with it. Way it happens, I've only got enough men to defend the jail. That's because most of the folk in this town made some kind of excuse when I asked for help. But like I said, I'm doin' the best I can. Now, about Sarah. I've spoken to nearly every man and woman in this town, and nobody saw the bushwhacker who pulled that trigger. You say it's Cole, but sayin' ain't provin'."

"That's a decent standard, Trey. In fact, Sarah made that same point only this morning. I just want to know why it doesn't apply to Francisco Rivera. You don't think he killed Elijah, but you're holdin' him for trial anyway. At the same time, you do believe that Cole wounded Sarah, but you let him go free. Where's the justice, Trey? Where's the justice?"

***

Josh sat by his wife's side once again in the early afternoon. There would be a mass funeral for those lost two nights before.

That would take place in just an hour, and Josh was expected to attend, to pray for the souls of the dead when he needed someone to pray for his own. He found himself returning again and again to a single question. If a man sins, knowing he's going to sin, knowing that he's going to offend the very God he worships, can he beg forgiveness later on?

And this was no little sin he contemplated. Josh had already attacked Uriah and his cowboys for playing judge and jury, citing the biblical story of the adulteress threatened with stoning to reinforce his argument. Justice among the Hebrew people, he preached, was reserved to judges only.

And now?

There was a further consideration as well, one that nagged at the back of his mind. He'd wandered in his own wilderness for many years, and now he was contemplating a return to that same wilderness. Who was to guarantee that he'd find his way home? Reformed drunks know they can never drink again, that a single sip of alcohol will put them right back where they started. And then there was Sarah. Could he do what he was contemplating, could he take Uriah Thorpe's life, take it in cold blood and remain the man Sarah married? Could he tell her what he'd done, or would he have to conceal it for the rest of their time together?

With no answer to any of these questions, Josh simply held his wife's hand. Sarah was still groggy but determined nonetheless. As a nurse, she'd witnessed the power of opiate painkillers, the power to enslave. Tens of thousands of the Civil War's injured veterans suffered from what had come to be known as the soldier's disease. These were men who craved the substance every hour of every day.

"I can't let myself become one of them," Sarah told her husband. "After today, no more."

"Why don't you worry about getting better?" Josh knew Sarah wasn't out of the woods yet. According to Carmelita, who was napping, the wound was inflamed, though not infected. A good sign, but it would be days before her recovery was certain.

"I'm more worried about you, husband. You have to stay above the fighting."

"Even if the town is destroyed in the process?" Josh shook his head. "This morning I counted twelve strangers—and there are probably more—ride into Whitegrass. Not cowboys, Sarah. Hardened fighters. Then, about an hour ago, Uriah and Cole followed them."

Sarah's strength seemed to leave her at that point, and she fell back against the pillow. But her voice didn't waver when she said, "We must all choose, Josh, between the things of this world and those of the next. There were men of God on every battlefield in the Civil War. They provided a spiritual refuge to soldiers on both sides. They did not fight."

***

The skies were already darkening by the time the funerals began. Dark below, the heavy clouds were tinged with a faint green that Josh associated with stagnant ponds. An intermittent wind followed the clouds, now stirring up dust devils on the prairie, then as suddenly gone, leaving an oppressive calm behind. Off to the west, the rain was already pouring down, accompanied by lightning strikes that seemed as bright as the vanished sun. Off to the east, a smoky-white cloud boiled up into the sky.

Josh watched four pine coffins lowered into four newly dug graves, his heart heavy as he contemplated this waste of life. He was expected to say something but found himself unprepared. Unprepared and perhaps unqualified as he pondered the crime of murder. Still, there was nobody else, nobody to speak for three boys who'd died with murder on their hearts.

As Josh prepared to speak, two men joined the few mourners—Uriah and Cole. This was to be expected, Josh had to admit. After all, the three ranch hands had worked for Uriah. Nevertheless, he felt himself instantly seized by a wave of pure hatred that ripped through his body. If he was armed . . .

Josh wasn't armed; the only weapon he carried was his own words. He began at the grave of Deputy Hank Potter, whose wife and children stood nearby, and he kept his message short and to the point.

"Hank Potter was a good man, Lord, a man who attended church on Sundays, a man loyal, above all, to his wife and his children, a man loyal to the town he served. I believe you can safely welcome him into Your kingdom. He gave his life defending the rule of law against the insatiable greed of an ambitious man. One man, Lord, who put riches above the lives of men like Hank Potter." Josh turned to the graves of the three cowboys. "And these boys, Lord, these other boys laid to rest on this day? You know what was in their hearts better than I, Lord, but I ask You to remember their ages. These were boys, not men, children easy to influence. When their boss set them on the killing path, when he plied them with liquor, when his . . ."

Josh's prayer was interrupted by a series of lightning strikes. Not far off in the distance, but only a few miles away. The summer monsoon was in full swing, and there'd be heavy weather tonight, maybe heavy enough to postpone the fighting. But come tomorrow, Uriah would still be Uriah, and Cole would still be Cole.

"These boys were used, Lord, with no more concern for their welfare than fox terriers set on a cougar. The man who sent them off stands here now, proud of the killing and fully prepared to send more men off to die tonight, fully prepared to have this little town burn until there's nothing left but ashes if it will further his ambitions. So, I ask You, Lord, to have mercy on these young boys whose souls stand before You, and to focus Your wrath on the truly deserving. I ask You to reserve your judgment to the man who took advantage of these children, who sent them to die."

Enough, Josh thought, but his anger refused to cool. He turned on his heel and stared directly in Uriah Thorpe's eyes, stared hard enough to cause the man to flinch. But not Cole. Cole's face was creased by a thin smile, as though he and the preacher were quietly sharing a joke.

***

With sundown only a few minutes away, Josh sat once more by his wife's side. Sarah had developed a fever, low grade but definitely there. And no matter how often Carmelita or Doc told him it was only to be expected, the terror that found a place next to the anger and hate already driving him, would not diminish. Josh didn't believe that he'd survive the loss of this woman he loved more than himself.

Josh watched Carmelita clean and rebandage Sarah's shoulder, refusing to quit the room. Doc had left the wound open, the better to drain, but the end result, if she survived, would be a terrible scar. Sarah seemed aware and afraid, as she looked from her husband to the terrible gash in her shoulder. But although she moaned from time to time, she didn't flinch. An experienced nurse, she knew what had to be done. Better to not make a fuss, to get it over with as quickly as possible.

Carmelita's hands moved with great assurance as she covered the wound with freshly boiled bandages. When she finished, she said, "Reverend, let me give you these minutes alone before I give her some more of the medicine. But, *por favor*, be quick, Sarah is in great pain."

Exhausted, Sarah had little to say at first. She'd examined her own wound carefully and there was no fooling her. Sarah was a beautiful woman, a midwestern beauty with cornflower-blue eyes, light brown hair, and just enough freckles sprinkled across her cheekbones to keep her out of the sun as much as possible. This was her not-so-secret vanity. Sarah often carried a parasol when she ventured forth at midday.

"It's ugly," Sarah finally said.

She didn't have to elaborate. Josh knew her too well. Too well to lie to her. One shoulder would be higher than the other, permanently, and she would move unnaturally as she dragged her damaged shoulder along.

"How can it be," Sarah continued, "that so much can be taken in so short a time? And for no reason."

"It doesn't matter," Josh finally said. "I love you, and I'll continue to love you. This . . ." He gestured to her shoulder. "This is nothing at all, not to me."

But if that was true, how to explain the rage flowing through his body, steady as a pulse?

They sat in silence for the next few minutes, Josh holding his wife's hand, until Sarah, knowing Carmelita would be coming in soon, finally spoke her mind.

"A part of me wants . . . revenge. Revenge, Josh. I want to . . . to balance the scales." Although Sarah's voice was weak, her strength obviously waning, Josh did not interrupt. "I think if we were simple . . . storekeepers? If that were true, I might even demand that you . . . give me this justice. An eye for an eye. But you've chosen a different path. You've chosen . . . the Lord's path. Now you must pray, husband. For your wife . . . and for the town. You must put your anger to one side . . . and pray."

CHAPTER 33

With Sarah sound asleep, Josh left Whitegrass Mercantile through the back of the store. A pack draped over his shoulder held a slicker he could button almost from his ankles to his throat and a single glove. If anything, the skies above him had grown more threatening, the storms out on the prairie more numerous and more violent, but time and place were not of his choosing. It was now or never.

Josh stayed low as he circled the town. Some of the lightning strikes were intense enough to replace the sun, and he didn't want his silhouette noticed by a stray gunman looking out through a back window. That made for slow going, and Sarah's words rang in his ears at every step. Josh tried to tell himself that revenge had nothing to do with his mission. The range war had to be stopped, and only a fool would trade the death of one man, Uriah Thorpe, for all the deaths sure to follow from tonight's battle. But then a verse from 2 Timothy rose, unbidden, into his mind.

"Share in suffering as a good soldier of Christ Jesus. No soldier gets entangled in civilian pursuits, since his aim is to please the one who enlisted him."

God didn't force Josh to join His army. Jesus didn't twist Josh's arm. No, as far as Josh could tell, Moses, Isaiah, Jeremiah, and the other prophets kept their distance as well. It was Josh who begged to enlist, who begged to wear the white collar. And now what? Josh deciding to muster out? Or Josh choosing to quit the fight, the one between God and Satan with the souls of men and women at stake?

The going was tedious, what with Josh at times on his hands and knees, but patience was a virtue Josh had learned as a sniper. You got yourself into position early and waited for a high-ranking officer to make an appearance. If none did, you killed anybody wearing an enemy uniform. In the midst of a pitched battle, that killing might go on for hours. And the killing was so easy. Laid back, hundreds of yards from the fighting and tucked out of sight, your rifle one of thousands firing at the same time, you killed without risk.

Josh was still at it thirty minutes later when he smelled smoke. Almost simultaneously, a river of short, dark shadows darted past, only the clatter of their hooves allowing Josh to put a name to the shadows. These were javelinas, spooked by the smoke, and they were gone within seconds. Out on the prairie, a wildfire shot looping tendrils of fiery embers far into the sky.

Suddenly, Josh found himself laughing. He imagined himself struck by lightning or burned to death or pounded into unconsciousness by hail before he ever laid eyes on Uriah or Cole. When he faced his Maker, would the fact that no sin was actually committed allow him to enter the Kingdom? Or would the Judge of All sentence him to hell based solely on his intent? Or perhaps the bigger sin lay in Josh's providing himself with the means to sin. Sarah had long ago asked him to be rid of the Whitworth.

Josh sobered up fast when a bolt of lightning smashed into the tip of a giant saguaro no more than three hundred yards away. The cactus exploded, shooting bits of pulp into the sky. It began to rain a few seconds later, not hard but steady enough for Josh to shrug into the slicker and pull the glove over his right hand. Sniping is a fine art, and the smallest things—like a half-numb forefinger exerting slightly more pressure than necessary—can make the difference between a direct hit and a clean miss when you're hundreds of yards away. The glove was of tightly woven, uncleaned, oily wool. It would keep his hand warm and dry until the time came.

Up ahead, Josh finally rediscovered the stand of prickly pear, dozens of plants bristling with thorns. It seemed, he thought as he settled in, as he took a small folding spyglass from his pack and focused it on the town's quiet street, that everything out here in West Texas had thorns. Josh ran the spyglass along the north side of the street, past the Bright Chance Hotel and the Red River Saloon. Nobody about, no one yet willing to brave the elements, though figures were visible through the Red River's oversize windows. Josh shifted the spyglass to the mercantile and his own home. A kerosene lamp flickered dimly on the far side of the curtains drawn across a second-floor window. Sarah lay in that room, helpless, while he, her husband, prepared to betray her.

Josh was fortunate in that he'd chosen the right spot. He lay on rock, not earth, which would have turned into mud before the two men came outside the Red River Saloon. Heads swiveling in unison, the pair looked up and down the street, taking their time despite the rain, then went back inside.

From where he lay, Josh couldn't see the front of the saddlery, but his view of the rear was unimpeded. Don Diego's vaqueros had attached a sheet of canvas to the back wall of the store, and maybe ten men were huddled beneath it. Lightning strikes, virtually continual, revealed that all were armed. The vaqueros knew what was coming and they were ready, as, undoubtedly, were the men in front of the saddlery, as were the men inside the Red River. Josh could almost smell the blood as he unwrapped the Whitworth, as he brought the stock to his shoulder. When he finally brought his eye to the rifle's telescopic sight, he found himself instantly transported. He was at Shiloh once again, atop a knoll later called the Hornet's Nest, firing down into the Yankees trapped on the Sunken Road. Again and again, until his shoulder ached, until his fingers went numb, until his eyesight grew blurred. The telescopic sight presented images unavailable to regular soldiers, heads blown apart, grapeshot fired from cannons slicing through Yankee flesh, exploding cannonballs lifting men into the air. He saw the wounded, too, the despair and bewilderment on their faces, as if they could not absorb their fate. He'd targeted them as well.

The words came to him then, the Lord's Prayer, sounding inside his mind as if there was no other sound to be heard, not the crash of lightning or the hollow booming thunder. And not the whole prayer, either, but a single sentence: *"Forgive us our trespasses as we forgive those who trespass against us."*

The meaning, to Josh, was as simple as it was unconditional. You must forgive in order to be forgiven. This was the essence of Sarah's entreaties. There had always been wars, and always men of peace. How easy it would have been for Jesus to abandon the adulteress, to dismiss this immoral woman, to leave her to her fate. How easy it would have been for Jesus to subdue the Roman soldiers who led him to the cross, to crush Pontius Pilate and Herod Antipas.

Josh found himself asking a question he might have asked earlier. Maybe you could justify killing Uriah by claiming—or at least hoping—to prevent greater bloodshed. That didn't apply to Cole. But when the door to the Red River opened at that moment and men began to spill out onto the boardwalk, Josh looked first, not for Uriah, but for his gunman.

He found neither. Josh didn't recognize any of the men milling about in front of the saloon, rifles in hand, and he thought for a moment that all the turmoil was about nothing. There would be no stopping these men by killing their leader, and no revenge, either. Then Cole emerged, head swiveling as he checked his flanks.

Josh removed the glove on his right hand, then put the Whitworth's sight on Cole's head about mid-face. The man's eyes were narrowed, his nostrils pinched, his mouth tight. Even when the raindrops began to fall from the brim of his hat, his expression remained steady. Cole expected to put his life at risk on this very night.

Uriah showed his face a few seconds later, remaining in the saloon's doorway and out of the rain. Josh shifted the Whitworth, focusing not on Uriah's head, but on his chest. As he did, the rain began to fall harder and harder, throwing a darkening curtain between Josh and his target. Josh told himself to pull the trigger. This is what he'd been waiting for all day, this fast-fading opportunity. Just tighten down, just apply these few pounds of pressure, and the man responsible for Sarah's gruesome injury—the man willing to destroy the lives of every man, woman, and child living in the town of Whitegrass, this man without a soul—will trouble God's creation no more.

It was already too late, already the view through the Whitworth's sight had been reduced to a shifting gray curtain, at first a vague silhouette still visible on the far side, then, finally, nothing. Josh might be five hundred yards from his target, or five hundred miles. He cursed himself for a time, cursed his cowardice, cursed his weakness, cursed every one of his life's failures. But then Sarah's voice sounded in his ear, as clear as if she were standing right next to him.

"Josh, we can make another baby, right?"

CHAPTER 34

Even as his brain reeled, as he cursed his own cowardice, Josh's heart rejoiced. He dropped the Whitworth, knowing he would never lift it again, that he'd somehow been saved, yet he continued to berate himself. He'd failed, even as he succeeded. His vows to God and to Sarah had been kept, but the town of Whitegrass was now at the mercy of Uriah and Cole. Maybe it wasn't his fault. Josh's suggestion, that the town's business leaders place themselves between Uriah's gunmen and the jail, had gone unheeded. And Sheriff Schofield was right, too. He'd begged for volunteers to defend the jail but had been turned down by just about everyone. But even if Josh's neighbors were ultimately responsible, Josh couldn't deny that he'd had the means to end the conflict before it began, had the means at his fingertips and done nothing.

The rain slackened for a moment, as though gathering momentum, then slammed down, the drops falling so fast they bounced off the soaked earth, reaching back toward the sky. Josh tried to shield his neck above the slicker with the brim of his hat. No good. Then he tried to stand, but a gust of wind staggered him. By the time he dropped back to his hands and knees, he could no longer see the town, not even an outline, never mind the lightning strikes.

There would be no battle on this night. Whitegrass was surrounded by violent storms, north, south, east, and west. Uriah would have to regroup because the men who'd come out of the Red River Saloon had surely been recognized for who they were, by the sheriff and the vaqueros, both. They'd carried rifles, but not torches. They'd come to fight, not to be slaughtered.

Josh's thoughts were interrupted by a sense both odd and familiar, as if, still a boy, his mother was awakening him from a deep sleep, calling his name over and over until he finally acknowledged her voice. Now, as his ears opened to the outside world, he heard, beneath the howl of the winds, beneath the pounding rain and the thunder, a deeper rumble, a growl almost, as though from some awakening beast. He looked out sideways, still trying to shade his eyes, but could see only the dancing lines of rain, rendered fresh by every bolt of lightning. Still, the rumble would not retreat, but only became stronger, the beast now on the move, insatiable, irresistible, unrelenting. Far or near seemed no longer to matter, only the great roar, coming from above and below, as the beast stretched its ravenous body.

Josh knew what was happening out there on the prairie, though some part of his brain refused to accept the reality. He needed to see, to confirm the obvious with his own eyes, as if not seeing might somehow turn the storm away. Then he did see, a darker twisting shadow within the shadows, leaping off the scrubland, dropping down again, always coming forward.

Unable to move his eyes or even to formulate a plan of survival, Josh could only wait. He could now see dozens of small black shadows flying in all directions liked spooked crows from a farmer's cornfield. The storm was lifting debris from the ground, plant and animal, stone and sand, and Josh was sure to be torn apart if the advancing storm crossed his sniper's nest, sure to join the dark shadows dancing in the tornado's revolving winds.

Josh's lips began to move on their own as he prayed, not for his own life, but for his wife, for her safety, then for the safety of the town, his friends, even for the armed camps on either side of Whitegrass's main street. Did the beast hear him? Did the Lord hear him? Or were his prayers too vague? Did they include too much? The tornado was close enough for Josh to follow its writhing length from the ground into the clouds, to know it as small, no more than forty yards wide, and moving very fast.

***

In the end, the tornado spared Josh as it cut through White-grass's heart, engulfing the Red River Saloon and the Bright Chance Hotel, the lumberyard and the hardware store, Judah's feed store and the saddlery, and a freight yard that carried heavy goods out to the farms and small ranches. The church, sheriff's office, the mission, and a few other businesses, their walls pitted as if by gunfire, remained upright. Everything else, every other building in the beast's path, exploded. They'd been thrown together hastily, and with materials hauled from far away. Now they went down in an instant that seemed to Josh, as he watched, an eternity.

Josh was on his feet and running, the Whitworth left behind, left forever, even as the storm's debris crashed around him. He was unaware of the danger, or even the destruction, as he plunged ahead. Still mumbling a prayer, though the words never reached his consciousness, he raced toward his home and his wife.

The debris settled within a few seconds, but the dust remained in the air for a longer time, preventing him from seeing what he most needed to see. Josh was within a hundred feet of his home before he found that his store and house were exactly as he'd left them, not a roof-shingle misplaced, even the windows intact. Still unsatisfied, he never slackened his pace as he ran through the store and up the stairs to find Carmelita at the window, staring out, and Sarah, under the influence of the laudanum, barely awake. Then he stood for a moment, his relief threatening to overwhelm him, as his fear had done.

When he'd steadied himself, Josh joined Carmelita at the window. The center of Whitegrass, Texas, was gone, replaced with heaps of rubble now being excavated by desperate men and women in search of survivors.

Josh hesitated just long enough to lay a gentle kiss on Sarah's cheek as he whispered a prayer of gratitude. Then he joined the rest of the town, men and women, Texans and Tejanos, who'd been spared. All worked side by side as the crushed and mutilated bodies of vaqueros and gunmen and ordinary town folk lay side by side next to the cistern. There was nothing new about any of this, not to Josh, who'd witnessed the siege of Atlanta. You set to work after a bombardment, lifting timbers, clearing doors and roofs, stopping often to listen for the muffled cry of a trapped survivor.

A long pry bar in hand, Josh uncovered his first survivor after only ten minutes when he levered a section of flooring off to one side. Bobby Drake, son of Charlie and Eva Drake, owners of the lumberyard, lay beneath. The boy, uninjured, stared up at Josh through beseeching eyes, his lips moving soundlessly. Only a few seconds later, Charlie held his son in his arms. His wife's body was already among those by the cistern.

The tornado had scattered debris and bodies unpredictably, and the work continued through the night. Beams and roofs had fallen a hundred yards out on the prairie, and Josh, shortly before sunrise, found himself searching through what remained of a storage shed that had been lifted, almost whole, from the pile of stones that had served as its foundation. The storms of the night had vanished, leaving crystal-clear skies behind, and the stars would have been enough, by themselves, to light Josh's search. Still, the better to avoid jutting nails, he'd added a torch, its shaft wedged between two splintered beams.

Josh listened first, lowering his ear to the pile, surprised to hear, faintly, the sound of a man breathing. As gently as possible, he lifted a piece of siding, glimpsing a human form below. Then he twisted the whole away, spinning it on one edge as he flipped it to the side. The sight that greeted him when he looked back was so gruesome that he again turned away. A man lay there, a man Josh would never recognize because his skull had been crushed and there was nothing left to recognize. Next to him lay another man, one he easily recognized as Cole Bradhurst, alive and alert. Cole wasn't moving, though, wasn't even crying out.

Josh retrieved the torch and held it over the gunman, examining him from head to toe.

"Can you move your legs?" he asked.

"No, sir. I cannot."

"Can you feel them?"

"No."

Cole's legs were crushed, as was his lower pelvis. He felt no pain because his spine was severed at some point. A blessing, Josh supposed, because the man was surely going to die.

"I didn't shoot your wife," Cole declared, the words spoken around a steady trickle of blood from the corner of his mouth.

Josh didn't respond at first, but he was impressed. He'd been slipping back as he tended the injured, reverting to the preacher he'd been prior to Sarah's wounding. Cole hadn't denied the attack on Elijah, nor his role in the massacre that had taken place the night before, only the shooting of Sarah. As if that alone provided salvation.

"I swear, Reverend," Cole repeated. "I didn't shoot your wife."

"I believe you, Cole." Josh found a man's hat only a few yards away. Cole's? Josh didn't know, but he flattened the crown and used it to cushion the gunman's head. He understood then, as he'd never understood before, that a dying man's soul was at stake. A dying man's soul and something more as well, a human life only half lived. The jail had been spared, and Francisco Rivera remained in his cell, awaiting trial.

"I believe you," Josh repeated, "but I don't see how it helps."

Cole shook his head, his blue eyes unfocused. "One time, we come upon an Injun family. Up in Montana. A buck and a squaw, their boy, a babe in arms, and their daughter. She was a pretty thing and the boys wanted to have some fun with her. I put a stop to it, Reverend. Left them people to go about their business."

Josh wet his bandanna with water from his canteen. He gave the bandanna to Cole, who brought it to his lips.

"Were you raised in the Lord?" Josh asked.

"Methodist."

"Were you attentive, Cole, to John Wesley's teachings?"

"Went so far as to be dipped in the waters at the age of thirteen." Cole stared up at Josh, his regretful eyes now far away.

"Baptized? Did you believe?"

"I did at the time, before the war."

"Then you know, Cole, that it ain't a balancing act, good deeds on the one side, bad on the other. It ain't about scales at all." Josh took the torch and ground it out in the dirt. The stars above seemed to leap out, actors awaiting their cue, the ribbon of the Milky Way a great arch that reached from horizon to horizon.

"Did you know Carmelita Mendoza?" Josh asked.

"The one that got religion and took up with Elijah Norton's wife?"

"That's her."

"I did, Reverend, from the Red River, but I never had no business with her."

"Well, I asked her about you and she told me you were a man who didn't know how to be happy. She said the worst of the others knew how to have a good time, but you brooded, Cole. Every minute of every day. She told me you were haunted by your past, that you couldn't get free, even for a few hours, even after a few drinks."

"Then I expect I'm gonna burn, Reverend. Because I'm dyin', right here and now, and there's no way of changin' the past. What's done is done."

Josh squatted next to the outlaw. In a way, the man was lucky. For men like him, early deaths were routine. But Cole was dying without pain, and that allowed him to look forward, even if he didn't like what he saw.

"It's not about deeds," Josh said.

"You know a back door, Reverend? A back door into paradise? Because, me, I can pick any lock."

Josh recognized the desperation behind Cole's joke and he simply ignored it. "It's about arms, Cole. Arms outstretched, reaching for you. It's about you reaching back. You remember that, surely, from your boyhood."

"Might be a bit late, Reverend."

"Not until you stop breathin'." Josh took the bandanna from Cole, wet it again, and passed it back. Above them, above the preacher and the dying gunman, a pair of shooting stars cut across the Milky Way. "I know you," Josh finally continued. "I see myself in you. And like you, I did good and bad things after the war. It wasn't only one way, though I will admit the bad outnumbered the good by a deal. I told myself, at the time, that I was beyond redemption, a hopeless case. So, why worry? Why even try to get yourself right with the Lord you believe in? Because you do believe, Cole, just as I believed, and you know it. So, the question answers itself."

Cole's gaze turned downward, toward his crushed legs. "You ain't part of this? That what you're tellin' me, Reverend? You ain't really in it?"

"That's exactly what I'm tellin' you. What's happening now isn't about you and me. It's about those arms I spoke about, the ones reaching out to you. It's about you and Him. But I won't leave you, Cole. I won't leave you to die alone, much as you may want to."

Josh reached into Cole's shirt pocket. He withdrew a cigarillo, placed it between Cole's lips, and lit it.

"You got work to do, Cole, and not a lot of time to get that work done. The well of sorrow, the one that kept you from enjoying the pleasures of the Red River and a hundred other bars? That sorrow is how your own conscience calls to you. It speaks with the voice of the Lord Jesus. Listen now, before it's too late."

Josh watched Cole nod, then resumed speaking, his tone matter-of-fact, as though repeating something Cole already knew.

"But there's somethin' else needs doin', and there ain't a lot of time for this, either. A minute ago, I believe I heard you go on about how you can't fix the past. What's done is done. That's what you said."

"You might wanna get to the point, Reverend."

"Point here is that you never said a word about the present."

"You mean about me gettin' torn apart?"

"No, I'm talking about a man sitting in jail, Cole, waiting to hang for a crime you committed. That's happening right now, even as we speak, and you have the power to put it right. In fact, I'd say you're gonna have a real hard time explaining your failure. Only a fool would ask the Lord to forgive a sin he's still committing."

Josh rose to his feet. He looked down at Cole for a moment, then drove in the last nail. "And, by the way. Your boss? Mr. Uriah Thorpe? He's safe and sound. In fact, he left for the ranch a few minutes after the storm came through. Now, I'm just gonna run over and fetch the sheriff. And while I'm not a Catholic, I do believe, this time, confession's gonna be good for your soul."

Cole reached out a hand to contain Josh for a moment. Although he grasped him with the hand of a drowning man, Cole was smiling that inward smile Josh had seen before. "Yeah, go do that thing," he said as he pulled on the cigarillo, as he let the smoke flow out through his nose. "Fetch Sheriff Schofield. And, Reverend, I promise to tell him the truth. I mean, it don't hardly make a difference, bein' as I won't live long enough to hang."

CHAPTER 35

The last grave, the last body lowered down, the last prayers. Josh folded his small Bible and lowered his head. The body belonged to a six-year-old boy named Thad McMartin. The boy had suffered a head injury in the storm, an injury that seemed at first negligible. Expecting him to wake at any moment, his parents had set up a vigil by his bedside. But Thad hadn't ever opened his eyes, remaining unconscious day after day, talking only sips of water, his small body wasting away, his parents forced to bear witness. Now he rested, sleeping the final sleep of the truly innocent.

"He's in God's arms now," Sarah said, as much to the boy's parents as to her husband.

Sarah's shoulder was healing well, due, almost certainly, to Carmelita's care. But Carmelita was gone now, back to Rachel and the Norton farm, whose healing wasn't healed. Sarah spent most of her days in pain, refusing any more pain medicine, fighting through.

"Thank you," Marla McMartin muttered. A small woman made smaller by exhaustion, she held tight to her husband's arm. Both husband and wife had worked at the Bright Chance Hotel—Solomon in charge of the kitchen, Marla in charge of the cleaning staff. They were humble people, the blessed meek, but they hadn't escaped the destruction. The innocent and the guilty, gunmen and vaqueros, old and young, male and female, all had found a place in the town's cemetery.

Josh took count of the mounds of newly dug earth, twenty graves. He'd prayed for all, one at a time, for innocent boys like

Thad McMartin and killers like Cole Bradhurst. Cole had given a full confession to the sheriff, then been asked to repeat it, this time with Pace as a witness. The gunman's confession included so many details, including Uriah's involvement, it could not be doubted. But Uriah remained one step ahead. Upon hearing of Cole's confession, he'd left the ranch on horseback for Austin. From Austin, he'd journeyed by train all the way to the East Coast, leaving Annabelle along the way. His whereabouts were now unknown to Sheriff Schofield, but it was assumed that he would not return. A replacement was already being sent to manage the properties, a man named Thurston Brown. The town fathers had yet to meet the man—he was due to arrive by stage in the afternoon—but he'd made his intentions clear by dispatching ten of his hands to help with the rebuilding.

The ten, still young enough to be called kids, appeared to be hard workers, as enthusiastic now as they were on the night they set out to hang Francisco. What thoughts had run through their minds when they learned that Francisco had been released, that Uriah had engineered the slaughter? Josh would never answer those questions. He knew only that Sheriff Schofield had opened Francisco's cell door on the night Cole confessed, then offered to escort his ex-prisoner out of town. Francisco had politely refused. Without assistance, he'd made his way on foot to the Norton farm and formally expressed his regrets to Elijah's widow. As far as Josh knew, even with the harvest all but complete, he was still there.

"Shall we go?" Sarah took her husband's arm, laying the tips of her fingers on the back of his hand.

Josh stole a glance at Cole's grave. The man had kept his word, honoring the obligation he had to other men. Had he honored his obligation to God? Josh had watched the man struggle as his strength ebbed. With his conscience? Or merely because he was afraid?

Fortunately, it wasn't Josh's call to make, and he turned toward the town, walking slowly, Sarah's good arm still entwined in his own. With Whitegrass far from rebuilt, the town folk swarmed around the construction sites, pounding, sawing, lifting. Several wagonloads of cut lumber had already arrived, sent from Austin with the encouragement of the governor. Other material arrived daily.

Whitegrass would survive.

***

The stagecoach rolled into Whitegrass at three o'clock, and one mystery was solved within a few minutes. According to Buck Rawling, the driver, Cole had met the stage only about a mile from the river on the day Elijah was murdered. Pace had been right, but nobody really cared anymore. Going forward, a can-do attitude, let the past be the past. This was the prevailing mood, one Josh fully recognized.

The town had come together after the storm, even those spared the storm's damage. Foundations were cleared and every scrap of usable lumber carried to a central point. The hardware store had been nearly destroyed, but its contents, the nails and hinges and screws and tools were priceless. Nails were gathered one by one.

The enthusiasm hadn't died out after a couple of days, or even a couple of weeks. The town would not only be restored, it would be reborn, bigger and better than ever. Thus, the interest in the man who stepped out of the stagecoach, Mr. Thurston Brown, new manager of Uriah's Bar-T ranch.

Everything stopped, including Josh, who stood in front of what would be the Bright Chance Hotel, hammer in hand. Thurston was a short man, no more than five and a half feet, with broad shoulders and the bow legs of a man who'd spent his life on horseback. He wore a gray suit, simply cut, over a white shirt with blue piping along the collar and pockets. His gray slouch hat had seen better days yet fit him like he'd been born to wear it. Most importantly, at least to Josh, his weather-beaten face was crisscrossed by hundreds of fine wrinkles, the mark of a man who'd passed his days in the sun and not behind a desk.

Thurston would not spend the night in town because there was no hotel to accommodate him, but he responded readily when asked by Pace to speak to the town fathers.

"Tell you what, Pace—I hope I can call you Pace—why don't I speak to everyone?" Thurston looked over at two cowboys on horseback. His cowboys. "Be along in a few minutes, boys."

The few minutes turned into thirty before Thurston stood on the boardwalk a few yards from Whitegrass Mercantile with the whole town lined up before him. Even Sarah had risen from the bed where she'd been resting. She now stood next to her husband in the store's doorway, her left arm supported by a sling, as it would be for many weeks to come.

"Well folks, my name is Thurston Brown." Thurston took off his hat and held it against his hip, the gesture seeming habitual. "I was born to the ranching life. Been on a horse since before I could rightly walk. Now I've been hired by the firm of Harris and Tweed in Dallas to manage the Bar-T ranch. I know there's been a heap of trouble in recent weeks, but that ain't rightly my business. No, my business is about cattle, the Bar-T's cattle, and nothin' else. I'll leave the rest to the sheriff."

A man's voice cried out from the crowd. "Where's Uriah Thorpe? The man ordered a murder." Josh thought the voice belonged to Charlie Drake, who'd lost his wife, but he wasn't sure.

"Don't know," Thurston said. "Thorpe ain't my problem. No, sir. Come September, I expect to drive a thousand head of cattle up to Nebraska. Plenty of problems there, as anyone ever been on a cattle drive already knows. Enough for me, anyway. But I got somethin' else to say, authorized by Mr. James Tweed, my superior in Austin. The Southern-Pacific railroad is comin' through your town in about a year. It ain't in writin' yet, but that's the plan, and there ain't nobody in Whitegrass or Austin who wants trouble before the deed is done. Best we should all get along, includin' the man named Don Diego. The whole of West Texas is openin' up, and there's room for any man's got the gumption to take advantage of an opportunity."

An excited buzz ran through the crowd, and Josh smiled to himself. Thurston, for all his homey approach, knew exactly how to placate the citizens of Whitegrass, Texas. The town would have to grow if it was to accommodate the railroad. Stockyards, first of all, to contain herds that would need water and feed. There'd be work aplenty for Pace, too, and for the dozens of cattle brokers who would negotiate on the part of slaughterhouses a thousand miles away. But just about every business in town would have to expand. A school would have to be constructed and a teacher hired. The town would need a courthouse, too, and a city hall and elected officers, a mayor, and a town council.

Josh felt the touch of his wife's hand on his shoulder. He turned and smiled at her.

"I used to think love was enough," she said. "But now I know human beings need something else."

"And what's that, Sarah?"

"The future, Josh. They need to believe in their own future."

Josh laughed. "And me, fool that I am; I thought that was my job."

***

Toward evening, Sarah closed the store and carried a basket packed with supper to where her husband labored over a fallen beam. Josh was busy trimming a splintered end, but he gladly quit when Sarah walked up. He took the basket, and the two strolled past the now-empty jail to their little church without exchanging a word. Circling the back of the church, they finally settled on the edge of the porch, looking out over the Pecos onto the prairie. The sun was setting behind the church, and its angled light cut across the tops of every tall saguaro, the luminous green as intense as any emerald.

Josh emptied the basket he carried, laying out the food, a beef stew loaded with carrots and onions harvested from the Norton farm. Two mason jars held cider brewed from dried apples and peaches.

"Josh," Sarah finally said, "there's something we need to talk about. Something I think I know already."

Recognizing her tone, Josh came near to choking on his cider. Sarah wasn't asking permission to speak. More like she was ordering him to give her words his full attention.

"Let's hear it."

"Your rifle, Josh, the one you brought with you from the war."

"The Whitworth?"

"Yes, the Whitworth. It's missing."

Josh stared off into the flatlands beyond the river for a moment, noting an armadillo poke its head out of a burrow, cautious, careful. Then he leaned over and kissed his wife, the kiss tender and lingering.

"It's probably a couple of hundred yards out that way." He waved his hand at a patch of cactus, maybe the one he'd used as a blind, maybe not. He was no longer sure and didn't really care. "I took it out there intending to seek revenge on Uriah and Cole."

"How odd, Josh. Instead of harming Cole, you tried to save his soul."

Josh listened to his wife laugh, feeling himself blessed to have the love of a woman with her strength. Their lives would go forward, the babies she longed for certain to come.

"I had Uriah lined up, Sarah. Had my sights fixed on his cold heart and my finger on the hard trigger. I already told you what I did in the war, so you know I wouldn't have missed if I had pulled down."

Sarah laid her good hand on Josh's elbow. "But you didn't."

"Couldn't. Like my finger was made of stone, like it wasn't meant to bend. Then the storm closed in and . . ."

Josh tore a small loaf of yeast bread in half, then passed a piece to Sarah.

"I knew when you left that night," Sarah said. "I wanted to go after you, but I was too weak. All I could do was ask the Lord to protect your soul. I told Him that you'd spent most of your life in search of His grace and would He be so kind as to not leave you on your own now that you'd found it."

Josh began to laugh. "That, my dear wife, comes very close to spiritual impudence."

"Does it?"

"Yes, it does."

"Well, I don't care because my appeal was heard, at least as far as I can tell. And you should rejoice, my husband, because you've been tested, taken right to the edge, and you stayed true. To Him, to me, and to our family to come."

Josh smiled. He took Sarah's hand, and together they gazed west to the enchanted sunset, a lowering circle of gold that threw ramparts of crimson and purple with an intensity that only the Master's hand could paint.

They watched the prairie settle before them and deepen into the shades of twilight—as beautiful and wild and mysterious as the Pecos itself.

CPSIA information can be obtained
at www.ICGtesting.com
Printed in the USA
BVHW071326200519
548789BV00004B/411/P

9 781593 309558